Her Faux Fiancé

Alexia Adams

Copyright

Her Faux Fiancé

By Alexia Adams
Copyright 2016 by Alexia Adams

Published by:
Alexia Adams
Suite 377
255 Newport Drive
Port Moody, BC V3H 5H1
Canada

Contact: Alexia@alexia-adams.com
www.alexia-adams.com

Edited by Julie Sturgeon
Cover design by Steven Novak

Ebook ISBN 978-0-9939126-5-8
Print ISBN 978-0-9939126-6-5

First ebook Edition January 2016
Second ebook Edition June 2018
First Print Edition February 2021
Product of Canada

Dedication

This book is dedicated to the people of Manitoba. You are an incredibly hardy people, and I am in awe of your strength and determination. I lived in Gimli for eight years and I learned a lot about myself during this time. The most important of which is that I am not strong enough to be a Manitoban. The bug-infested summers—even with their incredible sunsets late at night—weren't enough to overcome the long, dark winters with wind chills that make a polar bear think twice about stepping outside. I am weak. And that's why I now live on the West Coast. I may get moldy from the rain, but at least I won't freeze to death trying to get my car to start in -40°C because I forgot to plug it in.

Manitobans, I thank you for sheltering me in your midst during those eight long years and teaching me to run backwards so my nose didn't fall off from the wind chill (even though I did run into a parked car that one time). And for curing me of any bug phobia simply by overwhelming my senses with the sheer number of them. I now know never to wear a white t-shirt during fishfly season and how to get rid of ticks, important life skills I wouldn't have known had I not lived in Manitoba.

So, to all Manitobans, past, present, and future, I dedicate this book to you.

Acknowledgments

I want to acknowledge the warmth and kindness of the Icelandic community in Manitoba. You took a teenage girl with a thirst for knowledge, welcomed her into your incredibly rich culture, and rarely laughed as I tried to learn your mind-boggling difficult language. *Takk fyrir matinn* (because I can't remember how to say thanks for the lessons).

Of course, this book wouldn't be readable without the skill and genius of my editor, Julie Sturgeon. You make me sweat the words out, Julie, but it's always worth it in the end. I love you. (Ha, got it in before the book even started!) And here are a few extra commas for you to slip in where I've missed them: ,,,,,,.

And it would all be pointless if I didn't have readers like you. Thank you for spending your hard-earned money on my book. I hope you enjoy it! *Takk*!

Chapter One

Erik sped down the highway on autopilot. After 120 kilometers of farmers' fields, there wasn't much to attract his attention. His right foot eased off the accelerator as he approached the town limits. He slowed even more when he saw a silver SUV stopped in front of the welcome sign. His mind absently registered the rental sticker on the vehicle. Must be a lost tourist. Although there weren't many visitors who bothered to come this deep into the Canadian prairie.

An urbanite for the past decade, his every-man-for-himself thinking told him to keep driving. Another fifteen minutes and he'd be at his grandparents' farm. Quarter of an hour and he could relax with a beer after the two-day drive from Toronto.

The prairie boy in him, however, wouldn't let him drive past. "Help a neighbor in need" had been drummed into him for too long to ignore. Perhaps they'd run out of gas, underestimating the distance between towns. He pulled up behind the vehicle and shut off his own engine.

He expected the SUV's occupant to emerge from the vehicle, but when no one appeared, he hesitated. Maybe they were sick. Erik glanced at his cell phone. No service. If they were ill, he'd have to drive them to the hospital himself. He grabbed the mini first-aid kit from the glove box and raced over to the driver's-side window. A petite woman sat there with her head on the steering wheel. When she didn't notice him, he rapped on the window.

She leapt in her seat and screamed. Damn, he was supposed to be helping. If she wasn't having a heart attack before, she might be now. Regaining her composure, she turned the key in the ignition and then lowered the window.

"I'm sorry, miss. I didn't mean to frighten you…"

Blue-green eyes met his, and his heart started to pound. He glanced at his chest, sure she could see his reaction. The one person he thought he'd never see again. *Of all the roads in all the world, why did she have to break down on this one?*

"Analise?" Incredulity made his voice rise two octaves. He cleared his throat.

She blinked twice, a blank look on her face. What seemed an eternity later a small smile played about her lips, as though unsure what it was doing there. "Hello, Erik."

Two words erased ten years. He was twenty-one again, in lust with his sister's best friend. Then she'd run from him when he needed her most and … the illusion of love had been shattered. What the hell was she doing here now? A death had made her flee, another must have brought her back.

"I was sorry to hear about your grandmother."

"Thank you." A tear fell from her eye before she wiped the heel of her hand across her cheek. It was both surprising and uncomfortable. She leaned across and retrieved a tissue from her handbag, and he took a moment to check out the woman in front of him. Because that's what she was now, a woman. The girl he'd known all those years ago was gone. The long, black hair that had lured his hands to run through its silky softness had been cropped short. Now, it stood off her scalp in spikes, daring anyone to come near. Her full, luscious lips that had beckoned his kisses were chapped, and she bit her lower one as she wiped her nose.

But those eyes. They were still the same mesmerizing aqua that called to him to lose himself in their depths, the color enhanced now by a sheen of unshed tears.

A ray of sunlight glimmered on the mountain of diamond on her left hand. Erik's heart constricted before he had time to reason with it. It'd been ten years, for God's sake.

"You're engaged."

She stared at her hand as if unsure how the ring had gotten there. Had she been sitting in the hot car too long?

"Your fiancé didn't come with you, then?" The pressure in his chest increased.

"No." The answer came out a whisper. An entire saga untold behind the one word.

"Are you okay, Analise?"

She nodded and replied, "Yes, I'm fine. Thanks for stopping. I was just looking at the sign and marveling how nothing has changed in … well … forever."

He couldn't let her slip away again. At least not

until they had a chance to talk. He had ten years of questions for her. Why'd she leave? Why hadn't she trusted that they could get through the tragedy together? He deserved a few answers. "You've changed. Do you have a couple of minutes? How 'bout we have a coffee before you head to the stables? Is your grandfather expecting you?"

"He knows I'm coming today, but I didn't say what time I'd arrive. My flight plans were rather fluid. I really should get there, though, before he worries."

"Half an hour won't make much difference. Things *have* changed since you've been gone. It might help for you to know some stuff before you get to your grandparents' place."

Her eyes appraised him. She blinked once, shuttering her thoughts.

"All right. Rosie's still the only coffee shop in town?"

"Yup. I said there'd been changes, not a miracle." He laughed; she didn't.

He returned to his car and waited for Analise to drive off. If he went first, he didn't trust she would follow. And he needed to talk with her before she saw her grandfather. Now that he'd had a couple of minutes to get over the surprise, her arrival was an unexpected but not unwelcome development in his own reason for making the trek to Akureyri.

He had to make sure she stayed around. She wasn't going to run out on him a second time. He'd seen the flight instinct in her eyes. Those incredible eyes.

***

Analise raised her window and started the engine. Well, that was her plan well and truly ruined. She'd intended to drive to the stables and convince her recently widowed grandfather to come away on holiday. A chance for them both to heal. Her grandfather was the only person left who could make her feel loved.

She'd wanted to get in and get out without meeting anyone who would dredge up the past. She hadn't even crossed the town line, and already she'd been discovered. And by Erik, of all people. *Merde, why did it have to be Erik?*

She glanced up. It had always amused her that the *Welcome to Akureyri* sign was so far from town. Was it there to give travelers some hope that civilization lay ahead? Because from where she sat, you could see tomorrow coming and yesterday leaving, without a house or barn to block the view. Or had it been an optimistic placing, thinking the town would grow to reach it?

Population 853. The number of residents hadn't changed in the ten years since she'd left. No one new ever moved to Akureyri—except her, and that had ended in disaster. Even here, in the middle of nowhere, she sensed a thousand eyes on her. There was nowhere to hide in the prairies.

She cranked up the air conditioner. With the engine off, the temperature inside the vehicle had crept toward uncomfortable but hadn't quite reached the unbearable level she'd experienced the past month.

Summer in Manitoba had nothing on the Middle East.

As she put the car in gear, her engagement ring caught her eye. Damn thing. She should never have put it back on after what had happened. Jean-Claude and their fading relationship was another thing she could relegate to the past. A past that wouldn't stay forgotten. She'd spent ten years running from it, only to have it knock on her car window. A shiver ran through her despite the warmth of the July day. She should never have returned.

Or she should have come back sooner, when she was at a good place in her life, so the dark memories didn't overwhelm her. Until the past month, however, she'd been focused on work, keeping that part of her life in first place—the part over which she had control. Behind the camera she didn't feel, didn't get involved. She was there to document the action. Her career was an invisible force field protecting her from hurt. Protecting her from life.

Now, even that had been ruined.

So, she'd returned to the place where she'd known true, unselfish love—her grandparents' farm. If she listened to her head, she'd make a U-turn right there on the highway and drive back to Winnipeg. She could call her granddad and get him to come meet her. Instead, she glanced in her rearview mirror. Erik sat behind the wheel of a dark blue BMW convertible sports car. He caught her gaze in the mirror and motioned for her to go first.

Chivalry was the word that came to mind when she thought of Erik. He'd even asked her permission the first time he'd kissed her. A tiny flicker of happiness sparked to life—he'd been such a good kisser. She put her sunglasses back on so he couldn't read her eyes, sure her need for comfort was visible even from that distance. Erik was the last person she could ask for solace.

After checking her mirrors again, she pulled back onto the highway. The one good thing she could say about today was that the SUV she drove was a hell of a lot more comfortable than the heavily armored vehicles that had been her main mode of transportation for the last two years.

Ten minutes later, she parked in front of Rosie's on the Corner. The irony of the name—it was the only building not on the corner—was another quirk of the place. Akureyri was a one-street town: a diner, bakery, grocery store, hardware store, pharmacy, bank, and liquor store. There was a bar at the far end of the street, on the other side of the railroad tracks. Locals didn't consider it part of town.

Erik pulled up right behind her and was standing next to her SUV before she'd even grabbed her handbag. He opened the door as she unlocked it. Out of habit, she reached for her camera bag in the footwell of the passenger seat but left it there on second thought. Her camera was her trademark, and she was trying to be anonymous. Yeah, right. Like that was going to happen in a town with a memory for scandal longer than a prairie winter.

Sliding out from behind the wheel, she stood next to him, tentatively putting weight on her left leg. Had he always been this tall? His six feet of hard muscle dwarfed her measly five-foot-two frame. Erik put his arm around her shoulder as if to protect her from the road traffic. It was unlikely that the one car that passed every five minutes would strike her in the two seconds it took to get to the sidewalk. But his arm did feel nice. Maybe, for just a second, she could lean on him, absorb some of his strength.

A little bell jingled as he pushed open the door to the diner, ushering her inside. The smell of burnt toast and greasy fries assailed her nostrils. In the darker interior, she automatically put her left hand up to remove her sunglasses but quickly changed her mind as her eyes always gave her away. She had a pair of brown contact lenses she wore when not blending in could mean losing her life. Perversely, she wished she'd worn them today.

"Erik Sigurdson! I heard you were coming into town for your grandparents' sixty-fifth. And you've brought your fiancée with you. Hello, I'm Sheryl Kowalchuck." The waitress rushed over to them and held out her hand, the overpowering scent of Angel perfume nearly smothering them.

Analise shook hands with the other woman, biting her tongue. "Pleased to meet you," she managed to reply with a tight smile. How wonderful it would be if she could pretend she'd never met any of these people before.

Sheryl had tormented her almost daily for the three years of high school they'd attended together. Analise glanced up at Erik, waiting for him to refute the fiancée statement. Instead, he pulled her tighter against his side before he led her over to a booth.

She slid along the red, fake-leather seat patched with silver duct tape. The plastic menu Sheryl handed her had seen better days as well. A number of menu items were crossed out with black marker.

"Have we met before?" Sheryl gave Analise the once-over.

"People tell me I look like Anne Hathaway. Maybe that's why I seem familiar." She still had a faint hope of leaving with only a few people knowing she'd been in town.

"Maybe." Sheryl shrugged. She turned all her attention back to Erik. "What can I get you?"

"Just coffee thanks, Sheryl," he said.

"Coffee for me too, please." Analise handed the menu back to the hovering waitress, who seemed in no hurry to fill their order.

Sheryl kept her eyes on Erik. If Analise really were his fiancée, her claws would be emerging about now. "I heard you're a hotshot lawyer living in Europe. Must seem very small, coming back here." Sheryl's simpering little laugh grated on Analise's remaining nerve, which was perilously close to snapping.

"Akureyri will always be home," he answered.

While the waitress flirted with Erik, Analise took the opportunity to peruse her alleged fiancé. Ten years ago, he had been a tall, lanky college boy. His ready smile and mischievous blue eyes had her crushing on him from the first time they met. Now, he was all man. The lankiness had disappeared under muscles that would make a sports star proud. The glimmer in his eye was still there but accompanied now by the glow of experience, a look that said, "I know exactly how to please a woman—wanna see?"

Erik was most likely the best-looking man to set foot in this café in years. Analise smiled. So much for worrying about being recognized.

"Can we get those coffees to go? I want to show my fiancée around town before we head out to my grandparents'," Erik said as Sheryl continued to stare. He reached out and covered Analise's hand on the table. A current passed between them, and she saw his eyes widen as though surprised that after all these years the spark was still there. Even Sheryl seemed to notice.

"Oh, uh, sure. I guess we can catch up later. Almost the whole town is going to the big anniversary bash, so I'll see you there. Erik's grandparents were the first ones married in the local church," Sheryl said, her eyes flickering to Analise.

"Yes, he's told me."

Finally, Sheryl moved away. Analise opened her mouth to ask why he was pretending they were engaged when he lifted her hand, which was still under his, and kissed her knuckles.

"I'll explain in a minute," he whispered against her skin. She tamped down the shiver of awareness that ran from her hand up her arm and into her belly. He kept hold of her, toying with her engagement ring with his thumb. Pasting on a smile in case they were being watched, she pulled her hand away and edged closer toward the end of the bench. What kind of game was he playing? Was this some sort of payback for the way she'd left? Rubbing her nose in what could have been?

As if she hadn't thought about that enough in the past decade.

Sheryl returned two minutes later with Styrofoam cups. The Frenchwoman in Analise was appalled to see the treasured liquid subjected to such degradation. She'd had coffee served to her in gold-rimmed glasses in a Bedouin tent in the middle of the desert; who was to say what passed for civilization?

Erik pulled out his wallet, but Sheryl put her hand up. "It's on the house."

"Thanks, Sheryl. We'll see you around," Erik called out as they left the coffee shop.

As they stood on the sidewalk Analise looked left and right. Nope, not much had changed. The bank had a new coat of paint, and a bench had been installed in the empty lot next to the bakery. Erik led her toward it, his arm around her shoulder. The warmth of his hand began to melt the ice walls she'd built around herself to survive the past few weeks. And, given the spectacular failure of her plan to slip in and out of town unknown, she was likely going to need that protective wall in the near future. Because once she let herself feel, there'd be a flood of emotion to contend with.

"So, we're engaged? I thought I'd agreed to have a coffee with you, not become your wife. You work fast, Prairie Boy." Analise took a sip of her coffee and grimaced as the stale, bitter liquid scorched her tongue. She poured out the rest on the ground.

A full-on grin split his face at her use of the old

nickname. Sunshine glinted off his ripe-wheat colored hair, and ten years evaporated in an instant. "Yeah, sorry about that. I guess if you show up with your arm around a woman who's wearing a diamond big enough to put an eye out, people will leap to conclusions—the exercise of choice in this town."

She raised an eyebrow at him while her heart did that odd flip-flop thing. How could she ever have forgotten how gorgeous he was? Or the way he once made her feel—like she was the most important woman in the world to him? "That accounts for Sheryl's assumption, but not the fact that you didn't deny it."

"I wanted to see what if felt like to be engaged to you. We could have been, you know."

"That's the past, Erik. We can't resurrect it."

"Maybe it's just dormant, waiting for the two of us to get back together."

Analise doused the flame of hope that dared flicker to life in her chest. Hadn't her heart taken enough of a beating in the last few months? She couldn't let herself be deluded by the memory of a past romance. She'd moved on, become a different person. Undoubtedly, he had as well. Erik wasn't hers, never really had been.

Although, if Erik had been her fiancé, he might not have put her life in danger time and again. And she wouldn't be sitting here with a shrapnel wound in her leg and another man's ring on her finger.

Erik took her hand in his again. His strong fingers massaged the back of her hand. She closed her eyes and let herself enjoy the gentle caress. It had to be the exhaustion and pain warping her judgment.

"Analise, will you pretend to be my fiancée while you're here?"

The question startled her eyes open. She pulled her hand back. She should have known a man, even Erik, would want to use her for his own ends. "For what purpose?"

He ran a hand through his golden locks, making a curl fall boyishly across his forehead. Hadn't she learned by now how deceiving looks could be? There was nothing boyish about Erik.

"Every time I speak with my mother or grandmother, they ask when I'm going to settle down and get married. I'm here for three weeks. If they ask even once a day, it's going to drive me insane. We cared for each other once. I'm sure we can fake it now."

"Have you stopped to consider that maybe I've told my grandfather all about my fiancé, and you're not him?"

Erik stared into her face. "Have you?"

She closed her eyes again. She hadn't even told her grandfather about the engagement. Her relationship with Jean-Claude had been complicated from the start. In her rational moments, she'd realized she'd mostly stayed with him because it was better than being alone.

She opened her eyes to see Erik's gaze caressing her face, as though he couldn't get enough of looking at her. Or maybe he was trying to find the girl she once was. That wasn't going to happen either. *Come on, Analise, get your mind back in the present.* "No. But that's not the point."

"What is the point?" When he stared at her with those blue eyes, she had trouble remembering. Breaking his gaze, she kicked at a dandelion with her foot. The seeds fluttered away in the breeze as though they'd just been waiting for the chance to escape.

"Embarking on this charade is lying to our families." She'd had enough of lies to last her a lifetime.

"It's making our families happy for a brief time. It's my grandparents' sixty-fifth anniversary, and I don't want questions about my perpetual bachelorhood to spoil their celebrations. You know how they worry. It's just for a few weeks, while all the family is here. And I'm sure your grandfather would like to know that someone is looking after you. When we leave, we can wait a respectable time and then announce our breakup. Besides, there is another consideration."

She loved Erik's grandparents like they were her own. If she could do anything to make sure they had a fabulous family reunion... She couldn't lie to herself, though. Three weeks pretending to be Erik's fiancée was more temptation than she could resist. Her heart still equated Erik with happiness. And she sure could use some of that.

She cocked her head to the side and stared back at him. There was more to this story than Sheryl's assumption, although he seemed to have run with that. If Erik had really wanted someone to pretend to be his fiancée, she was sure the list of willing candidates would have been a wheat field long. So why her? Especially after what had happened. He clearly had another ace up his sleeve. As a photographer, she could read body language, capture elusive emotions. Erik was hiding something.

Searching his face, she dared to ask, "What else?"

"Has your grandfather told you anything about his business?"

"No, why? I mean, I know he's scaled back a bit and doesn't have as many horses."

Erik took a deep breath and let it out audibly. "He doesn't have any horses, except that old gelding of yours. The stables are in serious financial difficulty. The bank is foreclosing on Monday."

"What? Why didn't he tell me any of this?"

Erik shrugged.

Her grandfather was a proud man and not one who told the world his worries. Closing her eyes, she ran a hand through her hair. "How much to pay off the bank?" She was afraid of the answer.

"Around a hundred thousand dollars."

"A hundred thousand?"

Analise's mind whirled. If she sold all her assets, including her apartment and portfolio, she might be able to scrape that amount together. There was no way she'd manage that by Monday, though. "It'll kill my granddad to lose the stables, especially on top of losing Grandma." She had to save her grandfather, to atone for all those she hadn't been able to help.

"I have the money. I can go to the bank and make the transfer tomorrow," Erik said.

"How do you know all this?"

"One of my cousins works for the municipality,

another for the bank. Nothing is really private in a small town like this."

Don't I know it.

"So, I pretend to be your fiancée for a few weeks, and you settle my grandfather's debts until I can pay you back?"

"Exactly. Will you do it?"

"Why are you doing this, Erik? What would you have done if I hadn't decided to come back to Akureyri today? What if I had brought my fiancé with me?"

"You didn't, so why worry about what hasn't happened? Will you pretend to be engaged to me?"

"Can I think about it?" There was something he wasn't telling. Some other reason he needed a fake fiancée. Could she still trust him?

He glanced over her shoulder before putting his hand to her face. Lowering his head, he took her lips in a kiss so gentle she wondered if she'd imagined it. She was used to her mouth being ravaged. Erik's soft touch was like a taster, leaving her wanting more. The flicker of happiness grew a touch brighter.

He pulled back a fraction. "Enough time?" He nuzzled her ear, setting off a tingling sensation in her abdomen. "We're being watched."

Being watched was nothing new. The French government had let her go, but she was pretty sure they weren't done screwing with her life. Evidently, Erik was now a hotshot lawyer. Having someone with legal knowledge could come in handy. This could work to her advantage, too.

"Well, I guess it will be all over town within

minutes. And if I deny the engagement, it will lead to more questions." *Smile and nod and get out without telling them anything.*

"Thank you, Analise. You don't know how happy you've made me."

Enough to make up for the way I left before? They couldn't go back. But maybe they could part as friends this time. "Just don't expect too much. I'm not the girl I used to be."

"Neither of us are the people we used to be." His phone rang. Glancing down, he gave a wry smile. "It's my mother. That took longer than I expected." He answered the call on the fifth ring.

Analise twirled her engagement ring on her finger as she half listened to the snippets of Erik's mother's tirade. Jean-Claude would have understood her decision. He'd been all about doing what needed to be done in the moment—and dealing with the fallout, emotional and otherwise, later.

Erik's voice interrupted her musing. "It was supposed to be a surprise… Yes, Mom, we're on our way… No, you'll meet her in a few minutes. We just stopped to grab a coffee… Yes, I know you have coffee there. Listen, you won't be too clingy, will you? My fiancée isn't used to such a hands-on family. All right, we'll be there in twenty minutes."

He hung up and winked at her. "The show has begun. I guess we'd better go see our families now."

"I suppose." Analise had a terrible feeling this whole thing was going to turn into a right pain in the aperture.

"Do you mind if we see my family first? The farm is closer, and my mother might actually explode if she doesn't see us soon. We can leave your vehicle here and go the rest of the way in my car. We'll need the time to get our story straight."

She hesitated, and Erik put his hand on her face again, running his thumb over her chapped lips with a feather-light touch.

"*D'accord* … okay." She must've been tired; she tended to slip into French when exhausted. "I want to get a *vinnaterta* from the bakery for my grandfather before we go."

"No problem." Erik stood and waited for her. When she rose, he put his arm around her waist. Analise enjoyed the feeling of security. The air was filled with birds singing to each other, and a light breeze blew a gentle warmth against her skin. No bombs, no staccato gunfire. Just peace.

Well, and Erik.

Chapter Two

Ten minutes later, she sat beside him in his BMW, the cake in her lap. One hand was fisted on the seat-belt buckle, the other rested on the door release. She was more skittish than a newborn calf about to be checked over by the vet.

"I'm not going to hurt you, Analise. I will never hurt you," he said.

She took a deep breath, and he could tell she was forcing herself to relax. "I know. I just like having my own wheels."

His jaw clenched at the reminder—so she could run again if she wanted. But he needed her cooperation if his plan was going to work. At some point, they'd have to face the past. For now, though, they had to sort out a story good enough to fool his family. He was counting on the fact that bringing home someone they already knew and loved meant they wouldn't question why he hadn't told them about Analise before.

"I've been living in Europe for the last eighteen months. I assume you've been in France?" He glanced at her after he pulled onto the highway. She now clutched the cake box, but at least her knuckles were no longer white.

"Among other places. But yes, I've got an apartment in Paris."

"So we can say we met again when I visited Paris and have carried on a relationship for the past year or so, and we got engaged last week. Your fiancé's not likely to show up out of the blue, is he?"

Analise paled. "No, Jean-Claude's out of my life."

"Your engagement is over? Why are you still wearing the ring?" This was good news … for his plan, of course. He tried to keep the joy out of his voice and failed.

"We were together for a very long time. I guess I'm still coming to grips with the fact he's gone."

"I'm sorry." His smile disappeared at her evident agony.

"I'll get over it, eventually."

"I can see how hard this is for you." He paused and softened his voice. "Still, for appearance's sake, I wish you were wearing my ring…"

"You're not walking around with an engagement ring in your pocket, are you?"

He clenched his teeth. The answer to that question was going to take longer than the short ride to his grandparents' farm to explain. He kept quiet, hoping she wouldn't pursue that line of questioning.

Eventually, she asked, "So, you've been working in Europe. Whereabouts?"

Easier. *Keep to the facts, counsellor.* "London. I'm a mergers and acquisitions lawyer at Douglas and Wilder. They're based in Lincoln's Inn Fields, and I have a flat in Islington. What do you do?"

"I'm a freelance photographer. I've been working all over the world, mostly in Africa and the Middle

East. I haven't spent a lot of time in Europe the last couple of years, so if you get specific about places we've supposedly been, let me know."

"I've been working nonstop on a very large takeover bid for the past year and a half. I've only had a few weekends free. None of my family came to visit, because I couldn't get the time off to show them around. The merger finally went through last month, so I've got six weeks' leave. I plan on staying three weeks with my family, then I have a holiday booked in the Seychelles. How long will you be in Manitoba?"

"I had hoped to convince my grandfather to take a trip to Iceland with me. Aside from that, I haven't any definite plans."

How much did her broken engagement figure into her lack of plans? She was the girl who had run out on him. Maybe she'd had a taste of her own medicine this time. Deep down, though, he hated to see her hurting. Damn it, would part of him always care for her?

Erik pulled off the highway onto the dusty gravel road that led to their respective grandparents' farms. Two minutes up the road, he stopped the car.

"Forgot the way?" For the first time since she'd gotten into the car, she looked at him fully.

He reached out and took her left hand. "Analise, I know this is going to come across as insensitive, but … will you wear my ring? It doesn't feel right pretending to be your fiancé with another man's ring on your finger. Especially one as big as that rock. I've got money, but there's no way my family would believe I bought something so … ostentatious. Was your fiancé compensating for something?"

She stared at the diamond on her finger. "I think what jewelry I'm wearing is the least of our worries."

To his relief, she twisted the ring off her finger and then tucked it into her pocket. He dug into his jeans' pocket, pulled out a platinum band, and slid it on her finger. While the diamond wasn't as large as the one she'd been wearing, it was cut and displayed more elegantly. It suited her long fingers, and they both stared at it.

It fit.

His eyes met hers. Did she feel like she'd been slapped in the face by the past as well?

"Are you going to tell me why you have an engagement ring in your pocket?" There was a note of steel in her voice, like this was all too convenient for her to believe. But that was what made him a damn good lawyer—his ability to think fast and turn a situation to his advantage. He'd just never expected to do it slipping his ring on a woman's finger.

"That's a conversation that needs to take place over a couple of beers," he replied, forcing a note of humor into his voice. He restarted the car before she could demand an explanation. As she slid on her sunglasses, he noted the deep shadows under her eyes and the pain in their aqua depths. A twinge of guilt pinched his heart. He'd just conned an exhausted, heartbroken woman into pretending to be his fiancée. To make up for it, he'd play the part to the best of his ability. *High-school drama classes, don't fail me now.*

Five minutes later, they pulled into the long

driveway that led to his grandparents' farm.

"It's exactly the same," Analise said, a slight catch in her voice. "Nothing has changed." Was she remembering the last time she'd been there? He reached over and squeezed her hand lightly.

The light blue, single-story house with navy trim did look just the same. Baskets and planters surrounded the dwelling and overflowed with a variety of blooms in every color imaginable. He hadn't lied back in the café. This would always be home.

"Some things have changed—my parents are divorced, and my father recently remarried. He and his new wife are coming on the weekend for the family reunion and my grandparents' sixty-fifth anniversary. My mother is here as well, so it's bound to be very tense. That's one of the reasons I've come early, to support her."

"Your mother still lives in the same house?"

"Yes. She gets on with my dad's family better than my father did. Mom never really got over my sister's death. Sometimes she still talks as though Karen is alive."

"Oh." There was a depth of emotion in that one word he didn't have the energy to question right now. If Analise had stayed rather than run away…

He stopped the car, and before he had shut off the engine, his mother flew out of the house.

"Erik, Erik, oh, it's so wonderful to see you!" His mother launched herself at him as he stepped from the vehicle. The force of her embrace knocked him against the car door. This did not bode well. He'd been hoping for happy. This hug bordered on desperate. And he could smell the wine on his mother's breath.

Erik pulled out of his mother's arms and reached for Analise's hand. She'd gotten out of the car and stood to the side. There was an odd wistfulness to her expression.

"Mom, say hi to my fiancée. You remember Analise, Gunnar Thordarson's granddaughter?"

"Analise! Oh my God, I can't believe it's you. You're back. And with Erik. This is just so perfect. If only Karen were home. She'd be so happy. I'm so happy. I worried Erik would marry one of them snooty lawyer women and live in the city—or worse, in Europe. But now it's you. I knew ten years ago you two were meant to be together. And now you are. I can't wait to tell everyone. Come, sit down. I want to hear all about the wedding plans. You're going to get married here, aren't you? You have to. It's only logical with both families living so close—"

"Mom, stop. You're scaring her." He put his arm around Analise. She was so pale, he was afraid she might pass out any second. "Analise just got off a long flight, and I've been driving for two days. Give us a chance to catch our breath."

"Oh, Erik, you don't know anything about women. We love to talk about weddings, don't we, Analise? My goodness, I haven't even hugged you yet. Welcome to the Sigurdson family." His mother wrapped Analise in a hug so tight he heard the air whoosh out of her lungs.

"Mom, enough."

Reluctantly, his mother released Analise from the

bear hug.

"Thank you for the welcome, Mrs. Sigurdson."

"We're family now. You must call me 'Mom.'"

He hadn't thought it possible Analise could turn any whiter. She swayed on her feet and grabbed his arm. "No, I can't."

Oh God, this was going from bad to worse. Not only had his mother brought up Karen but now another tragedy from Analise's past. If he wanted to keep this fiancée play going more than ten minutes, he had to get her out of here.

"I want to go to my granddad," she said in a strangled voice.

Her obvious distress brought out his protector instinct. He'd put her in this situation, now he had to get her out. Erik took her hand, opened the passenger-side door, and helped her in. Her muscles were coiled, ready for flight. Would she always react to trouble by running away? He needed to remember that so he didn't repeat the mistakes of the past. She was too much of a flight risk to gamble his heart on her again...

"Erik, where are you going? You can't leave. You just got here." His mother's voice rose, and she reached for the wine glass that she'd abandoned on the porch railing.

"I'm taking Analise to her grandfather's. I'll be back in a bit," he called out.

He glanced over at Analise as he started the engine. Her bottom lip was caught firmly between her teeth. "I'm sorry about my mother," he said as he pulled out of the driveway and onto the dirt road that led to her grandfather's stables. "She drinks, and she's caught up in her own little world. I'm sure she just forgot about your mother."

Analise released a weary sigh. "It doesn't matter. But I don't know if I can take all the wedding talk. Not so soon after..." She stared out the window. As they passed the fence that marked her grandfather's land, she turned to Erik. "Can we end this farce now? If you'll lend me the money for my granddad's debts, I'll repay you as soon as possible."

"I vote we keep the engagement going. I just need to talk to my mom, and she'll calm down. Besides, Sheryl will have told the whole town by now. What will people think if we break it off so soon? Please, I don't want a scandal to mar my grandparents' anniversary."

It was low, playing on her affection for his family. But he wasn't ready to give up on this yet.

**

She closed her eyes. The world was conspiring against her. Her planned escape from life to heal her body and heart had now turned into a fraudulent public exhibition of a love she'd long ago put into a mental file called "things I've lost." It was a fat file.

But the senior Sigurdsons had always treated her as though she were another granddaughter. They'd celebrated every achievement with her, giving her congratulatory cards when she'd gotten her driving license or aced a test. And every year on the anniversary of her arrival in Akureyri, they'd baked a cake, bought her presents, and partied like it was her birthday. A few weeks of pretending to be Erik's fiancée would hardly repay their years of kindness. "*Eh oui*, all right, as long as it doesn't upset my granddad. He's my first priority."

"Agreed."

They pulled into her grandparents' driveway. Through a blur of unshed tears, she noted the white siding needed a clean and the red trim had faded to a dingy pink. Her grandmother had always kept the house and garden immaculate, and Lara Thordarson had been famous for her white geranium arrangements. When Analise had first left Manitoba, she'd put a drop of geranium oil on her pillow every night to help her sleep.

Now a few dead lobelia and dried up pelargoniums hung out of forgotten baskets. The grass in front of the house was yellowing and knee-high. She'd dreamt of her homecoming so many times. This wasn't what she'd seen in her mind. She blinked rapidly, not wanting Erik to see her cry.

The car bounced up the rutted drive, bottoming out on some of the larger potholes. Erik grimaced at a particularly nasty scraping sound.

"We should have brought the SUV," Analise said past the lump in her throat.

"I'll get it with one of my cousins and bring it to you."

"Don't bother. Granddad and I will collect it later."

"It's not a problem."

"It is for me. Granddad and I will collect it later."

Erik shot her a look, but she wouldn't relent. She had the feeling he wasn't used to people saying no to him, in business or personal matters. Well, he'd have to get used to it. Jean-Claude had called all the shots for the past four years. Analise was going to live her own life from now on.

Except she'd stupidly agreed to play the part of Erik's loving fiancée for the next three weeks.

I guess the compulsion of doing everything to please others is going to be harder to break than I expected.

He pulled the car to a stop in front of the house, yet no one emerged from the dwelling. She dragged her weary body out of the car and climbed the three steps to the wraparound porch, not realizing that Erik had come to stand beside her until his arm went around her shoulders, giving them a gentle squeeze. Her heart pounded, and without his support she might have swayed. The doctor had warned her not to do too much too soon. Evidently, flying for eighteen hours and then driving for almost two counted as too much.

She walked around the porch to the kitchen entrance then stopped. Should she knock? Just go in? This had been her home for three years, but it wasn't anymore. Before her knuckles could make contact with the peeling paint on the door, it opened. She blinked to adjust her eyes to the dim light inside the house. Her grandfather stood before her, his shirt missing a button, a brown stain on the collar. His clothes hung off him as though they'd been purchased three sizes too big.

Gunnar Thordarson was a large man. Analise had always imagined he was what Vikings had looked like. Now his shoulders stooped, his hand shook as he ran it over his messy beard, and his once lively blue eyes were murky, almost gray. Still, when he caught sight of her standing at the door, he opened his arms wide and swept her into a hug.

She choked back a sob against her grandfather's chest. Thirteen years ago, when she'd been exiled to this corner of the world, thousands of kilometers from anywhere and anyone familiar, her grandfather had taken her in his arms and promised to be there for her. His love and her grandmother's had gotten her through one of the worst periods of her life. Now she needed to be there for him.

"Welcome home, sweet." Gunnar's gruff voice still boomed in his chest.

Analise stepped back but kept hold of her grandfather's hands. "It is *so good* to see you, *Afi*." The Icelandic term for grandfather rolled off her tongue without a second thought.

"Hello, Mr. Thordarson," Erik said. She had forgotten he was still there.

Her grandfather looked the younger man up and down, a frown creasing his brow until he seemed to recognize who it was. "Erik Sigurdson?"

"Yes, sir."

"What are you doing here with my granddaughter?"

She smiled. Evidently, old habits were hard to break for everyone, and her grandfather had immediately slipped once more into a protector role.

Erik put his arm around her shoulder again and waited for her to look up at him. "Aren't you going to tell your granddad, love?"

Love? Erik really was taking this role of fiancé seriously. Her real fiancé had never even called her that.

"Tell me what?" Gunnar crossed his arms over his chest. He might have lost weight and shrunk some, but he could still appear intimidating.

She hesitated until Erik squeezed her shoulder. She'd made a deal; it was time to play her part. "We're engaged," she said, trying to inject a note of enthusiasm into her voice.

"You didn't mention this on the phone," her granddad accused.

"The phone line was terrible. I could hardly understand a word you were saying. And I thought it would be better to present Erik to you in person." She swallowed on the lie.

"Well, if you're happy, I'm happy. I take it you'll be staying over at the Sigurdsons', then?" Gunnar's shoulders fell again, and the animation that had come over his features at seeing her disappeared.

"No, I'm staying here," she said quickly. "I mean, as long as that's okay with you, *Afi.*"

A smile lit up his face once more. "Of course it's okay. This is your home."

Analise turned back to Erik. "I'm exhausted, *chéri.* I'll see you tomorrow."

Erik nodded, but before she could turn away, he

put a hand on her chin and tilted her face up for his kiss. His lips pressed a gentle caress against hers. It was stupid because she knew it was all just part of the act, but it made her feel special—something she hadn't experienced in an awfully long time.

"Sleep well, my love. I'll be by in the morning." Erik saluted Gunnar; then, jumping from the porch, he climbed into the BMW, leaving a trail of dust as he drove down the long drive.

Mon Dieu, *what have I got myself into now?*

Chapter Three

Erik turned up the music and tapped against the steering wheel in time with the country beat. If he'd planned it for years, today couldn't have turned out any better. He was on the verge of crushing his enemy. And pretending to be Analise's fiancé meant he got to kiss and hold her whenever he wanted. Which, face it, was no hardship. She was even more beautiful than he remembered.

He'd been infatuated with Analise from the first. She'd come to live with her grandparents following the death of her mother. Straight from Paris, the young French girl had seen the tiny town of Akureyri as the worst kind of exile. With her exoticism and beauty, she hadn't been welcomed by the other local teenage girls. She'd also been tarred with the same brush that had painted her father as a bad lot when he'd seduced and got Gunnar's teenage daughter pregnant. The fact that Analise was the innocent result of that bad behavior didn't seem to matter to the town gossips.

His sister, Karen, who had always been on the outside of the popular cliques, had latched on to Analise, and the two had quickly become best friends. Erik had been away at university at the time and only met Analise after she'd been in Manitoba for several months. He could still remember the pain in those uniquely aqua-colored eyes and the vulnerability in her smile.

Over the summers he'd spent on his grandparents' farm, he'd gotten to know her—her quick laugh, shy smile, and the way she'd look at him when she didn't think he was watching. She'd been interesting to talk to, as well. Having lived in Europe, she had a different outlook than those he knew who had never been beyond the Manitoba borders. And she'd been so sweet to his family, helping out in the house when his mom or grandmother were ill, making birthday and anniversary cards for his grandparents as though they were her own. Laughing at his father's awful jokes.

Yeah, they'd been good times. For God's sake, he'd been excited just to get up in the morning, knowing he'd see her that day. And morning joy was nothing on the nights he'd spent dreaming about her in his bed.

When he'd come back to the farm for his sister's graduation ceremonies, Analise had turned eighteen, and he'd been unable to resist her any longer. And to his immense relief, she seemed as into him as he was to her. The kisses they'd shared had lingered in his memory for years.

He'd intended to see her grandfather and ask permission to start dating his granddaughter. After the scandal surrounding her parents' marriage, Erik wanted to ensure their relationship was aboveboard. Unfortunately, he had to go back to Winnipeg the following day for an interview, and by the time he'd returned, everything had changed.

But that girl was gone. The few smiles he'd seen from her today had been tinged with defiance. She was definitely tougher now. So why did he still want to take her in his arms and tell her everything would be all right? When he knew that, until he'd sorted out the past, nothing would be right.

For now, however, they were pretending to be engaged, and he was damn sure going to enjoy it.

He pulled into his grandparents' drive to see his mother sitting on the porch swing, the now-empty glass of wine still in her hand. Okay, there was a tiny flaw in the day. Stopping the car, he took a deep breath and went to talk with her, hoping she wasn't too drunk. He'd failed his sister; he couldn't let his mother down as well. He didn't blame his father for leaving, but it meant Erik was the only one left to pick up the pieces.

"How's it going, Mom?"

She raised blurry eyes to his. "I'm sorry, Erik. I forgot about Analise's mother. Now I've ruined everything." A sob caught on a hiccup.

Erik sat next to her on the swing, moving the empty bottle of wine out of the way. "You haven't ruined anything, Mom. You just need to back off a little. We're newly engaged, that's all, and we haven't discussed wedding plans. We're here for Gran and Gramps' sixty-fifth. Let's just concentrate on that for now. Okay?"

Because he wasn't going to even fictitiously plan a wedding with a woman who ran the second things got tough.

Besides, he had other things to concentrate on

while he was here. Like making sure the man responsible for Karen's death paid the price.

Yes, he'd fix the past, enjoy the present, and then figure out what he wanted for his future.

***

Analise stepped down the narrow hall and walked back in time. She opened the door to her old room, automatically stopping the door before it creaked.

She might as well have been eighteen again. The room hadn't changed. Posters of Arabian stallions and long-forgotten pop stars still adorned the walls. A hairbrush and curling iron sat on the dresser, waiting to be called to action. She noticed a small vase of daisies next to the bed. Her grandmother had always kept fresh flowers in every room, even in winter. There were none left alive in the garden. *Afi* must have made a special effort and bought some just for her.

"I hope it's okay. I washed the sheets, but I'm not very good at making beds, so you might have to fix it."

"It's wonderful, *Afi*. Thank you," she whispered. A lump was stuck in her throat.

"I'll let you rest now. Then maybe we can get some dinner at Rosie's when we go to pick up your vehicle."

Her grandfather backed out of the room and closed the door behind him.

Analise sat on the bed, sinking into the soft mattress. A framed photo of her and Karen was propped up against the bedside lamp. She picked it up and ran the tip of her finger over her best friend's face.

What would my life be like if Karen had lived? If I had stayed on in Akureyri? Worked with Afi *in the stables? Married Erik and had his babies?*

A tear trickled down her face and landed on the glass covering the photo. She had to be more tired than she'd thought for the tears to fall so freely. Flipping the photo over, she released the clips at the back and removed the cardboard holding the glass and photo in the frame. Sandwiched between the backing and the photo was another, smaller picture. One she'd stolen from her best friend.

Erik looked so much younger, yet her heart rate still accelerated when she saw his face. He'd been her first love, the reason she hadn't gone with Karen to the party that ultimately led to her death. Instead of celebrating with her fellow grads, she'd stayed at home and prepared for her first proper date with Erik. After he asked her granddad, they were going to drive into the city and, well, dinner and a movie weren't the only things on the agenda.

Putting the photos away in the bedside table, she shut off the memories. Wishes wouldn't change the past, or the future for that matter. She grabbed her handbag from where she'd slung it on the bed and searched inside for the vial of antibiotics. A swig of water from the bottle she'd bought at the airport helped two of the pills down.

She bit her bottom lip as she eased her jeans past the large bandage wrapped around her upper thigh. Thankfully, there was no sign of blood or oozing. Still, it hurt like heck. Wishing she'd also filled the prescription for painkillers, she lay back on the bed and covered herself with the homemade patchwork quilt, wrapping herself in her grandmother's love.

***

The room was dark when Analise woke. A faint shaft of pink light came through the gap in the curtains. A glance at the clock revealed it to be five thirty in the morning. She'd slept for over twelve hours. The pain in her leg had lessened to a dull throb, and her stomach protested the lack of food.

Gingerly, she climbed out of bed and opened her duffel bag, instinctively stepping over the floorboards that squeaked. *Afi* must have brought her things in while she slept. Next to the bag sat her camera cases. She would have loved a shower but didn't want to wake her grandfather at this early hour. Pulling on a pair of yoga pants and a t-shirt, she made her way to the kitchen, hoping to find a cup of coffee and a slice of the *vinnaterta* she'd bought yesterday.

The enticing aroma of fresh-brewed coffee filled the kitchen. Next to the pot sat the cup she'd always used as a teenager and a slice of cake covered in plastic wrap. Analise filled her cup, added a spoon of sugar, and leaned against the scratched and worn wood counter. A rhythmic *squeak* came from the porch. Opening the door, she found her grandfather sitting on one of the rockers, watching the sun rise over the neighbor's wheat field. The soft, pink rays turned the still-green crop a dusty rose color.

Her grandfather turned his head at her arrival and motioned to her grandmother's rocker next to his. She hesitated a moment. *Afi* and *Amma* had always sat in these rockers, waiting for her to come home from school. Then, she'd sat on the porch railing and told them about her day. Even the memory brought peace to her soul. Yet it seemed wrong somehow to take the empty seat.

"I hope I didn't wake you," Analise began.

"No, I don't sleep much these days."

"*Afi*"—Analise waited until her grandfather looked at her—"if I had known *Amma* was ill, I would have come home right away. I would've been here for both of you. I'm so sorry. I didn't know."

"It's all right, sweet. We didn't even try to contact you until the doctors said there was no hope. Then that lawyer man told us that you were somewhere in the Middle East and he hadn't heard from you in months."

"My—colleague"—she stopped herself just in time before saying fiancé—"Jean-Claude and I were working on a story about the nomadic tribes of the desert. We didn't go to any towns or cities for several weeks. I should have kept in better contact."

At least that's what I thought we were working on. Turns out, I had no idea who my fiancé really was until it was too late.

"It was better that way. Toward the end, your *amma* didn't look like she had when you were here. It's good you remember how she was before."

"But I wanted to tell her how much I loved her,

how much I love you both. You're my only family."
Analise took a drink of her coffee, hoping to melt the
lump that had developed in her throat.

"She knew, sweet, we both did. What about your
family in France? Has something happened to your
father?"

"He's still alive as far as I know. I don't see him. If
we have to, we communicate through my lawyer."

"He is your father, Analise."

"He stopped being my father when he sent me
here." She could never understand how her grandfather
could be so open-minded and forgiving, especially after
what her father had done to her mother, Gunnar's
daughter.

"It all worked out for the best. We got to know and
love you, and you had a good life here, didn't you?"

"Yes, *Afi*, a very good life. That was because of
you and *Amma*. Not because of *him*."

"Well, despite the loss of your mother, we were
grateful to have you. We wouldn't have had it any
other way. And now you have Erik. I thought you were
seeing some French journalist?"

"I was, but then I met Erik again…" She stared out
across the land, not meeting her grandfather's eyes. She
hadn't lied, not quite. Was the guilt that skidded
through her from minimizing Jean-Claude's place in
her life or deceiving her grandparent? A soft sigh
escaped her lips. Analise reached across and took her
grandfather's hand in hers. Together, they watched the
dawn turn into day.

A day that would include Erik Sigurdson.

Chapter Four

"You're Analise Tagan," Sheryl accused. The waitress plonked the menus down in front of them. The complimentary glasses of orange juice received only slightly better treatment. "I knew you looked familiar, and it bugged me all day. So I checked my high school yearbook when I got home last night."

"It's Thordarson, now," Analise corrected. Sheryl looked perplexed. "I changed my last name when I returned to France."

"I didn't know…" Gunnar put down his menu, his blue eyes unusually bright when they met hers.

"I was going to change it to Gunnarsdóttir, but I figured I'd be spelling it constantly, and it doesn't really work outside of Iceland."

Sheryl shifted her weight from one foot to the other. As they weren't discussing Erik, she obviously wasn't interested. "Can I take your order?"

"I'm going to have two eggs over easy, bacon extra crispy, and whole wheat toast." Analise snapped her menu shut. "*Afi?*"

Her grandfather placed his order and handed the menu back to Sheryl.

"Why'd you change your name?" Gunnar placed his hand on hers. The weathered, callused palm felt wonderful.

"Because I consider you and *Amma* my parents. The Tagans never treated me like family."

"You shouldn't blame your father too much. He was sent to Manitoba by his family when he was seventeen because he got some bigwig's daughter pregnant in France. Your mother was all over him from the minute he arrived. It was inevitable that he would take what was offered so willingly. When his family found out he got another girl pregnant, they insisted he marry this time. I wish I had insisted they didn't marry, but your mom was so happy."

"Really?" Analise couldn't remember her mother ever being happy. At least not sober and happy.

"I think she was at first—the grand adventure, moving to Paris, seeing Europe. When we spoke on the phone she always said how great things were. We didn't know how bad it was between her and your dad. When she visited, she always seemed so bored and wanted to go back to France right away." Gunnar shook his head.

Analise didn't want to discuss her mother. That wound had healed, or at least scarred over so much it didn't hurt anymore.

Sheryl brought their coffees, hopefully a fresher brew than the last time. Analise took a tentative sip and managed to swallow without her taste buds revolting too much.

"So, *Afi*. As there doesn't seem to be much going on at the stables, I thought maybe we could take a trip to Iceland. See the real Akureyri together."

"What about Erik?" Her grandfather's question

came on the heels of Sheryl arriving with their breakfast. She lingered at the table, no doubt wanting to hear Analise's answer.

"Can I have some more orange juice, please?" Analise handed over her empty glass and waited for the waitress to leave.

"I'm sure he can spare me for a couple of weeks while I accompany my grandfather to his homeland." Quick save—she'd forgotten she was supposed to be engaged to Erik.

"I don't know. And we can't go right away. The Sigurdsons would never forgive me if I took their favorite grandson's fiancée away during their anniversary celebration. I have to live next to them."

Damn, there'd be no escape for the next three weeks at least.

"Well, think about it. We can go as soon as all this anniversary nonsense is over."

"Sixty-five years of marriage is not nonsense. It's an achievement to be celebrated. Not many young people nowadays can make a commitment that long. You think you and Erik have a shot?"

"I hope so." She meticulously put jam on her bread, hoping her grandfather didn't see the deceit in her eyes.

"Well, speak of the devil."

Before Analise could ask what her grandfather meant, Erik slid into the booth next to her.

"Good morning, my love." Erik turned her face up to his. The spicy scent of his aftershave filled her head seconds before his lips touched hers. His kiss was soft but effective. It scrambled her brain.

"Morning," she murmured as he pulled back a couple centimeters.

"Good morning, Erik. What can I get you?" Sheryl suddenly appeared at the table.

"I'll have the works," he declared. "I seem to be extra hungry this morning."

While Sheryl filled his coffee cup, Analise studied the man next to her. Dark denim clung to the hard thigh pressed against hers. A light blue T-shirt stretched across his chest, the color highlighting his eyes. Her heart fluttered a moment before a glint off her diamond ring reminded her that it was all a charade.

"Did you sleep well?" Erik's deep voice set the flutter off again. Her body was already betraying her. Heaven help her if they were alone for long.

"Yes, thanks. And you?" She sounded more like a distant relative than a lover. She'd have to work on her fiancée skills.

"Not really, I missed you," Erik said.

The implication heated her cheeks. *God, when was the last time I blushed? This past meets present thing is really getting to me.*

"I went by the stables," he continued. "But as neither vehicle was there, I figured you'd come here. You should have called me."

"Sorry. I thought your mother would keep you tied to her all day. I was going to stop by on my way back to Granddad's," she said.

Sheryl appeared with Erik's breakfast accompanied by a hot, lingering gaze. Analise couldn't really blame her. He was gorgeous. Even if he didn't want to fend off his relatives' comments on his continual bachelorhood, he probably needed a fake fiancée for protection. All the single sharks in town were circling the waters at the sniff of fresh meat. Analise shot Sheryl a "back off, he's taken" glare. Might as well start practicing her fiancée skills on her former nemesis.

Catching the interaction, her grandfather chuckled from his seat across the table. "What do you two have planned for the day?" He'd already finished his breakfast and drained the last of his coffee.

"Analise and I are going to set up a joint bank account," Erik replied before she could.

"Here?" A huge smile lit her grandfather's face.

"Yes. Even if we don't end up living here full-time, we'll visit often enough that having a local account will make sense." Erik's smooth explanation made it sound like they'd discussed all those mundane things a couple who had spent a lot of time together would have covered. Had he done this before with some other woman? After all, he'd had an engagement ring in his pocket; he must have been near a proposal with someone. But she couldn't really ask with her grandfather across the table and big-ears Sheryl hovering at a nearby booth. Another mystery to solve. Now all she had to do was not get caught up in the feel of his arms around her next time they were alone and remember to ask.

Two hours later, Analise wondered if they'd ever be alone again. After breakfast, they walked over to the bank, but with no line, Erik's cousin who worked there had assisted them quickly. Rather than set up an account, however, Erik had paid off her grandfather's debts and arranged for a small line of credit, with him acting as guarantor. The bank manager had then called her granddad to let him know that because he'd been such a good customer in the past, they were going to hold off the foreclosure and provide some capital to help him get back on his feet again. On Erik's insistence, his generosity was kept secret.

But she knew.

As soon as that was done, they'd run into virtually everyone from Erik's family who wanted to say hello. Then his phone rang, and his mother had pleaded with him to come home. Not ready for another meeting with Susan so soon, Analise had begged off and driven her rental SUV back to her grandfather's. But not before Erik had kissed her a lingering good-bye in full view of half the town. So, that was the engagement publicly announced. There was definitely no backing out now.

***

Analise slammed the phone down on the hook, intercepting a worried glance from her grandfather.

"Something wrong, sweet?"

She cast a puzzled look at her grandfather then remembered she'd been speaking French and he hadn't understood any of her phone conversation. Probably a good thing, because she'd let some rather rude words fly and her granddad had never tolerated swearing in his house. He might have given her permission, though, if he knew the reason for her distress. The goddamned French government had frozen her bank accounts and put a hold on her property and photography portfolio, rendering her virtually penniless while they investigated how much she knew of her former lover's activities.

"Just a hiccup with the bank in France," she prevaricated. "I'm sure it will all be sorted soon."

"Oh," her grandfather replied, a blush staining his cheeks.

With his own financial worries lifted, already she could see a rise in her granddad's spirits. His shoulders weren't as slouched, and his eyes held a little more optimism in them. She owed Erik. Big time.

And that didn't sit well with her. She hated being beholden to anyone, even her faux fiancé. But instead of a quick transaction to sell her flat and other assets in Paris, it now looked like it would be weeks before she could settle accounts. Added to that, as she had only purchased a one-way plane ticket, she didn't have sufficient money to fly back to Paris to sort it out herself.

Jean-Claude was still screwing up her life.

"I'm going for a walk." She grabbed her camera bag out of habit and strode from the house. She needed to get somewhere she could scream without further worrying her granddad.

Passing the empty stables, she headed for the furthest paddock. Thor, her old horse, raised his head as she marched by, then continued munching on a juicy patch of grass. The verdant blades were more interesting than the girl who had flown all over the countryside on his back in a futile attempt to run away from herself.

When she reached the far corner of her granddad's property, safe for now, due to Erik's generosity, she sat on a fallen tree trunk. Often, as a teenager, she'd lain on the ground here, staring at the clouds that passed overhead. How ironic that she'd become like one of those clouds—blown around the world at the whim of one man. She'd never realized the power and control Jean-Claude had over her until he was gone. Gone but not forgotten. Which brought her right back to her dilemma.

Away from everyone, she let the tears fall. She cried for Jean-Claude and their lost relationship, which, although troubled, had kept her from feeling alone. She cried for her grandma, who had always said tomorrow would be better. From where Analise lay, tomorrow looked just like today and yesterday.

When there were no more tears inside her, she wiped her face with her lens cleaning cloth. Wallowing in pity wasn't going to make it better. She needed to get her focus back. Work had kept her relatively sane for years. It had to help now.

Grabbing her camera, she aimed the lens at a butterfly resting on a wild rose blossom, the blue of the iridescent wings a beautiful contrast to the soft, pink flower. Her fingers automatically adjusted the focus and aperture, catching the moment when the insect rose majestically from the flower, fluttering its wings as it went in search of more delicious nectar.

A hawk soared overhead, searching for an unwary rodent for lunch. The lens she'd used for the butterfly photo wasn't long enough to capture the details on the bird. Reaching into her bag, she switched lenses without taking her eyes off the hawk. Animals weren't her usual subject, but it made a relaxing change from the despair and violence she normally captured.

After snapping a few more shots, she felt around in her bag for the lens cap. When she pulled it out, it slid out of her hand and into the long grass. Putting the camera on top of her bag, she went in search of the protective cover. As she kneeled down she heard a snap. Typical. Well, she had several spares in her other bag. She picked up the broken plastic shards and was surprised to find a piece of paper sticking out from one of the bits. Examining the fragment closely, she realized a false backing had been put on the original lens cover and a piece of paper inserted in the gap.

Analise wiggled the paper out, careful not to tear the delicate note. It was almost transparent, the thinnest tracing paper she'd ever seen. A few faint squiggles in pencil were barely visible. She grabbed her macro lens, installed it, and took a shot of the paper against the backdrop of her dark bag. Then she viewed the image on her camera screen. The note still resembled a bunch of squiggles but in an organized pattern. Staring at the photo for several minutes brought no enlightenment.

A light breeze flipped the paper over on her bag. She snapped another photo and examined the image again. The markings looked more recognizable.

Enlarging the image more, it suddenly made sense. Her breath caught in her throat, and her heart rate sped up. It was Jean-Claude's version of Arabic script. With his perverse sense of humor, her late fiancé had always written his notes from left to right rather than the proper way. Without the diacritics, it took Analise twenty minutes to decipher the message. While she could speak Arabic with some fluency, reading it had always proved more challenging, especially written backwards.

If you're reading this, Ana, call Mahmoud Abidjan
Then a Yemeni phone number.

As if she didn't already have enough governmental problems. Ringing an unknown contact in Yemen left to her by her dodgy spy lover would probably bring every antiterrorist organization in the western hemisphere down on her head. Still, Jean-Claude had put the note there on purpose. He'd undoubtedly foreseen what a mess he'd leave her in. She didn't dare call from her grandfather's landline. Seemed a trip to Winnipeg was on the week's agenda.

She tucked the paper into a hole in the lining of her bag and repacked her lenses and camera. Everything back in place, she got to her feet. A bead of sweat tricked down her cheek, and she wiped her forehead on the short sleeve of her T-shirt. Wishing she'd brought her hat and a bottle of water, she swung the camera bag onto her shoulder. She was so used to its weight, she often found herself going to adjust the strap even when she wasn't carrying the bag, like some people tried to push their glasses up their nose when the eyewear sat on the table next to them.

A shadow loomed in front of her, and Analise put her hand up to shade her eyes. Erik stood no more than two meters from her.

"You've got to stop sneaking up on me," she snapped. Her heart pounded, but she didn't know if it was from Erik's sudden appearance or just the fact that he was there.

"Sorry. I was going to call your name but thought that would frighten you as well. Are you normally this jumpy?" Erik reached out and grabbed the strap of her bag; instinctively, she clutched it closer. He raised an eyebrow and waited. Releasing her death grip, she let him carry it for her.

"Not usually. I guess I'm still jet-lagged."

"When I came by the house this morning and you weren't there, I thought you'd left. Again."

This was going to come up and bite her in the ass during every conversation if they didn't clear the air now. "Erik, I am truly sorry I left without saying good-bye."

"Why did you leave? We were on the verge of something great. If you'd have stayed, we could have faced Karen's death together. It would have made us stronger."

"I left because I felt guilty for Karen's death. I was pretty sure that in time you would see I was to blame. And I couldn't bear to watch what we were to each other wither and die when you realized it was my fault."

"Christ, Analise, how could you feel guilty? You weren't to blame. You were her best friend." He raked a hand through his hair.

"And as her best friend I should have done more. I should have stayed with her after school that day. I knew how upset she was. If I'd been a better friend... If I'd come over earlier..." *Instead of wasting time curling my hair because I wanted to look good for you.*

"Stop right there. No one blamed you."

She shook her head, trying to rid herself of the memory, but it was too strong. "Do you remember her funeral?"

"Yes."

"I stood there in the pouring rain across from you trying to comfort your mother, and it hit me that I was the common denominator. First my mother. Then Karen. Two people I loved, both gone. I had to leave before anyone else I loved died."

"Analise..."

"I was eighteen, Erik. Finding your sister ... it was too much for me. I had to get away. So I went back to France. I got counselling. And by the time I could face both those deaths rationally, you'd already gone to Toronto to start your law career. You had a new life, and all I had was emotional baggage. I thought I'd make something of myself so when we did meet again, I'd have something to offer. But then my career took off, and I figured you'd long forgotten about me."

"I never forgot about you."

"But you were better off without me. Look at you now—a top lawyer, the world at your feet. You've become an amazing man, Erik."

And she was still dealing with dead loved ones.

Chapter Five

"Analise, can you pass me the flour?"

She put down the knife she'd been using to slice cabbage and passed the requested item to Tracy, Erik's cousin's wife. They were putting the final touches on a meal for the immediate family. Just a small gathering of fifty.

Overwhelmed by all the people, Analise had sought sanctuary in the kitchen. Tracy, originally from a small family herself, had taken pity on her and kept her occupied. Erik's mother had popped in from time to time but left the bulk of the work for the two women to do.

"Do you think there's enough?" Analise surveyed the plethora of dishes on every surface. There was enough food here to feed an entire African village for a week. Everyone had brought something with them, so only a few last-minute items remained to be prepared.

"You haven't been to a Sigurdson family event before, have you? There won't be a lot left over once this bunch get their plates loaded." Tracy tasted the gravy she was stirring. It passed the flavor test, and she poured it into the waiting gravy boats.

Analise took a deep breath through her nose. Garlic, onion, and vinegar fought for dominance over the more subtle scents of cinnamon and paprika. She poured the mayonnaise mix on the chopped cabbage and stirred the coleslaw. As she was checking to make sure the cabbage was evenly coated with the sauce, a pair of strong arms wrapped around her waist. Her body tensed, and she grabbed the knife. Only when she recognized Erik's aftershave did she release the blade and relax.

One dead fiancé is bad enough. Two, and people will start to talk.

"Something smells fabulous," Erik said.

"It's the food," she answered. Her heartbeat slowly returned to normal only to speed up again when his lips pressed a soft kiss on her temple. How could Erik, with one small gesture done entirely to keep up the charade of a loving fiancé for his family, make her want him despite her better judgment? Had to be another inexplicable reaction to the recent upheaval in her life.

"It's not food I'm craving at the moment," he replied. His lips found the sensitive spot below her ear. Analise let her head fall back on Erik's broad chest. Why was she fighting this attraction? After all of Jean-Claude's lies, she owed him no loyalty. Perhaps she should melt in Erik's heat and mold herself into a new woman.

"Are the tables set up out there?" Tracy's voice broke through the fog of contentment that had invaded Analise's brain. When was the last time she'd actually been happy?

"Mmm-hmm…" Erik replied, his lips tracing their way back to her temple.

"Shoulda known better than to ask a man on the

make," Tracy said with a laugh. She wiped her hands on a towel and headed out the back screen door.

"Alone at last," he whispered.

"Yes, so you can drop the play-acting," she replied. Although her body protested, she wiggled out of his arms.

"You never know who's watching. It's better if we stay in character." Erik reached for her again, but Analise managed to avoid his grasp.

"Make yourself useful and take some of this food outside," she directed. If she was going to escape this pretense without further damage to her heart, she had better keep in mind that it was all a game.

"Not even married yet, and already you're bossing me around." Erik heaved a dramatic sigh; however, he picked up two laden platters and headed for the door. As he passed, he planted a kiss on her cheek. The feel of his lips against her skin lingered long after he'd disappeared outside.

All by herself for the first time in hours, Analise slumped onto a stool. Her original plan had been to slide into town, convince her grandfather to go on a brief holiday, then crawl into her Paris apartment and hide from the world for the next six months. Instead, she was neck-deep in family, pretending to love someone she hadn't seen in ten years.

And for once she didn't want to be anyplace else.

The back screen door slammed, and a steady stream of Erik's relatives entered, each picking up a plate, bowl, or container, and exited. Within five minutes, the kitchen was empty of food, and she could hear a chorus of voices calling various children's names to come and eat. She knew she should go out and join the crowd. Yet her feet wouldn't move.

Putting her crossed arms on the counter, she rested her head.

Next thing she knew, Tracy tapped her on her shoulder. "If you want to be more comfortable, you can lie down on the bed in the spare room."

"How long have I been asleep?" Analise stretched. She couldn't believe she'd fallen asleep on a stool with her head on the breakfast bar. She'd never been so exhausted in her life.

"About twenty minutes. Erik had to, uh, help his mother with something. He asked me to check on you."

In the hour before Analise had sought asylum in the kitchen, Susan Sigurdson had downed at least three glasses of wine. No doubt Erik was helping his mother sober up before his father's arrival.

"Sorry. I know you must be busy looking after your children. The last thing you need is to babysit me."

Tracy pulled out the stool next to Analise and sat down. "My kids are playing with their cousins. Besides, there are half a dozen moms to keep an eye on them."

"When Erik said this was going to be a small family dinner, I thought maybe ten, fifteen relatives."

"It's a bit overwhelming, isn't it? You'll get used to them. And if you need a break from all the noise, just pop into one of the bedrooms and hide under the coats. Don't go into the bathroom, though—with this lot and two toilets you'd be lucky to get five minutes."

Analise smiled. "You're not from around here, then?"

"Lord, no. I'm from Kenora. I know, not a big town either. But compared to Gimli or Akureyri, it's a metropolis. I can't imagine how you must have felt coming from Paris to here." A faint blush swept up her face. She must have been told of Analise's exile. Before Analise could reassure her that sensitive topic was ancient history, Tracy continued, "What's Paris really like? I've always dreamed of going there. We were supposed to go for our fifth wedding anniversary, but then I got pregnant."

"It's hard to be objective about Paris when you live there. As a tourist, it's beautiful and romantic. As a citizen, it's constant strikes and noise and, sorry to say, visitors clogging up the Metro and crowding in front of the masterpieces in the Louvre."

Tracy seemed a bit disappointed.

"But on a warm spring evening, you can pick up a baguette from the *boulangerie*, grab some cheese and a bottle of red wine from the grocery, and head over to the Champ-de-Mars. From there, you can watch the sun set and the lights of the Eiffel Tower twinkle in the dusk. If that doesn't appease the soul of the most romantic, then I don't know what will."

"That's why I chose it as the spot to propose." Erik's deep voice behind her made Analise jump.

She glared up at him. "I'm going to put bells on you so you stop sneaking up on me."

"Better yet, stick by my side, and I won't have to

sneak up on you." His arm wrapped around her shoulder, pulling her against his body.

"Erik! Erik!" His mother's wail caused the smile on his face to falter.

"I guess Dad has arrived. Come with me?"

"I'll be out in a moment," Analise said.

What would Erik's father say about his son's alleged choice? Would he be as forgiving of her sudden disappearance as the rest of the family?

***

Having hauled a few more bales of straw from the barn for guests to sit on, Erik searched the crowd for Analise's dark hair amongst the predominantly blond crowd. This was just the preliminary family reunion, immediate relatives only, and already his grandparents' farm was overrun with people.

When he'd introduced Analise to his father and stepmother, his dad's face had paled for a moment, but then his father had given her a hug and welcomed her to the family.

Erik's eyes finally lit on his pretend fiancée.

A shot of heat seared his intestines before taking up residence further down. God, she was beautiful. Why hadn't he followed her when she left ten years ago? *Because you thought she'd be back, that she just needed a little time.* He'd been so caught up in his own grief at losing his sister, he hadn't realized the trauma Analise was going through. To be the one to find his sister's body after what had happened to her mother—

no wonder she'd needed to go away and get counseling.

But here they were again. And *déjà vu* was doing a number on him. As much as he tried to resist, tried to focus on his plan to ruin the man who was truly to blame for Karen's death, he found himself drawn to Analise like he'd been in the past. He enjoyed her company, her quick sense of humor, and her appreciation for simple things—like the picnic on the beach yesterday. She'd been as happy munching sandwiches on the sand as other women he'd dated had been eating in a Michelin-star restaurant. Analise was no longer the girl who'd left him. She'd become an intriguing, beautiful woman he wanted to know better—much, much better, if his body had its way. Some things hadn't changed.

Right now, she was pouring lemonade into cups for a group of children. The smile she gave his cousin Brent's daughter didn't reach her eyes. She played the part of his fiancée perfectly, except there was a sadness about her that didn't jibe with the role of a happy bride-to-be. Most people had put it down to the recent loss of her grandmother. But he wondered how much had to do with the end of her engagement. And he intended to find out. First, he had to get someone else to support his mother so he could disappear for a while.

"Mom, I think Gran wants to speak with you." Erik steered his mother over to where his grandmother was waving at them. He mouthed the words "thank you" before striding over to Analise. She saw him coming this time, so she didn't jump at his arrival.

"You look like you could use a break. Come with

me for a few minutes." He took her hand and guided her away from the drinks table.

"But—"

"No buts. We're an engaged couple sleeping at our respective grandparents' places. People will expect us to sneak off for some alone time."

"But—"

Erik spun her into his arms, put one hand on her face, and kissed her until she clung to him. It was meant to be a distraction tactic; however, it resulted in wiping all rational thought from his mind. Good thing all he had to think about at the moment was getting Analise alone. Raising his head, he caught grins on a few of his cousins' faces. With his arm around her waist, he led her toward the barn.

Her steps faltered as they neared. "No, not in there." Her voice was filled with anguish, her face drained of color.

The barn. His sister's body. No, definitely not there. He bypassed the large, red building and strolled toward the trees at the back of the vegetable garden. Although planted to form a windbreak to protect the farmyard, it had been the perfect place to play as a child. Sure enough, a dozen or so children were either climbing the trees, yelling at others already up in the limbs, or trying to dislodge balls caught in the branches.

"There's ice cream and cookies back at the house," Erik announced.

The chorus of shrieks and squeals could probably be heard from the neighboring property. Within a minute, the woods were vacated. Pushing through the bushes, they came into a barren circle. A bed of leaves carpeted the area. He sat on the ground, his back against the trunk of a large silver birch and tugged on Analise's arm to join him.

"Bring all your girlfriends here?" she asked as he directed her onto his lap.

"You're the only fiancée I've brought here."

"Well, I guess that's something."

He raised her face and kissed her soft lips, his hands running up and down her crossed arms until he felt her relax against him. Resisting the desire to make her melt, to take the longing that hummed through his veins to its natural conclusion, he contented himself with holding her. He needed to know what happened to her previous engagement. He couldn't romance her if another man still held prime position in her heart.

Time to find out what he was up against.

**

Dieu, being held by Erik was becoming her addiction. His broad, muscled chest against her back, his strong arms around her... It was heaven. And rather than making her feel weak and small, she felt powerful, as though she were absorbing his strength. Most importantly, however, she felt cherished and cared for. Which was ridiculous, because it was all a sham. Too bad her body hadn't got that memo.

With her back to his chest, she felt as much as heard his words. "How are you coping with my family?

Anyone being too nosey?"

"No, everyone is very nice. A few remember me from … before. If this is just the immediate family, how many are you expecting for the full reunion next week?"

"A couple hundred, at least. Don't worry, we've hired some caterers to look after a lot of the food management, so you won't be stuck in the kitchen."

"I didn't mind." And she didn't; helping was part of who she was. She needed to be needed. That was something that had been missing from her relationship with Jean-Claude; she'd never sensed that he needed her.

Erik took a deep breath, and she steeled herself for his next remark. "I know you don't have much family… Did your ex-fiancé?"

Here it is, the interrogation about my previous engagement. "No, he was an orphan. That's one of the reasons we connected." Except Jean-Claude had never wanted family. Something that had begun to come between them the longer they'd been together.

"Tell me about him," Erik prompted.

"Why?"

"Because you seem so sad. And I want to help, but I can't unless I know what happened." His voice was soft and gentle, coaxing the story from her.

The French government should try this interrogation technique—have a sensitive man cuddle the informant. It was way more effective than sleep deprivation and ice-cold showers.

"His name was Jean-Claude."

"Why did you break up?"

"Because he died. I wasn't woman enough for him to live for." A shudder wracked her body, and he tightened his hold.

"You are more woman than most men can handle, Analise. What happened?"

"Turns out I never knew him. Our whole relationship was a sham." *Sound familiar? Maybe I've found a new career path—fake fiancée to manipulative men.*

"How long were you together?"

"Four years. It started out as a working relationship. He was a freelance journalist." *Or so I thought.* "I was a freelance photographer. We teamed up and worked together. It was a successful partnership. His articles and my photos sold to newspapers and magazines throughout the English- and French-speaking world. It was constant travel; as a situation died down, we'd move on to the next global hotspot."

"Sounds exciting."

"At first. Then we switched from reporting famines and natural disasters to conflicts and political unrest. And the constant worry about being kidnapped or killed… Stress eats away at the excitement until all that's left is fear."

"Why did you stay? Surely there are less dangerous places in the world to take photos."

"Of course. Jean-Claude thrived on the danger, though. He lived for the adrenaline rush."

"Even though you were scared? Surely he could

find some other way to get his thrills. Wasn't your safety and peace of mind his first concern?"

"No, it was always the job. The world needed to know what was going on, and we were the ones to tell them. It was my photos and his evocative words that made people give to charities for the starving and maimed children. It was my photos of dead babies and his brutal assessment of a situation that got the UN involved and prevented further bloodshed."

"Is that the line he fed you?" His voice vibrated with anger, but his touch was gentle. He twirled his engagement ring, which now sat on her finger. Was Erik regretting giving it to her? Had Jean-Claude begun to regret their engagement, like she had? They'd grown apart, wanted different things from life. He'd wanted adventure, she'd wanted stability. Yet, despite the arguing, they'd stayed together. He'd hung on because he was stubborn like that. And she'd been afraid to be alone. Now she knew there were worse things than being alone.

"It was true. We did good work. And I learned to control my fear. It made me cautious and probably kept me alive."

"And Jean-Claude?"

"He had no fear. The few times we were between assignments, he'd go base jumping or whitewater kayaking or climb frozen waterfalls. I was sure that was going to be the way he died."

"How did he die?"

Analise swallowed and rubbed her upper thigh. The pain was almost gone, but the memory was still fresh. "We were in Syria, in Aleppo. Jean-Claude had a rendezvous arranged with someone. The coalition forces were shelling the neighborhood where they were to meet. Snipers were outside the building where we'd taken shelter, and we could hear intermittent gunfire as soldiers shot anyone they found."

Erik's fists were clenched, his muscles bunched against her back. Did he want to hear the rest? Now that she'd started, she wanted to get it off her chest. "He went to the meeting?"

"I begged him not to go, to wait until morning. But he insisted it was vital that the meeting take place. He left, and I hid myself under some broken furniture. The soldiers did come in, but by then it was dark and they didn't see me. The next morning, when it seemed calm, I went to the meeting place. His informant was dead, shot in the head. Jean-Claude lay in a pool of blood, phasing in and out of consciousness. He had a bullet in the spine and was paralyzed from the waist down. I tried to move him … and he bled out as I held him in my arms."

"Oh God, Analise. I never imagined."

"You know what the worst thing was?"

"There was one worst thing? The whole situation seems a nightmare."

"I had imagined such a thing happening for so long that when it did, I didn't feel anything."

"And now?"

"Now, I feel it all."

Chapter Six

Erik rubbed his chest as his cousin at the bank gave him an update over the phone. Analise's revelation two days ago about her fiancé's death had left him unnerved. Faced with such trauma, his present course of action seemed childish. *I'm doing this for Karen.* But the tragedy of his sister's passing no longer had the same motivating force it once had.

"Erik?" His cousin's voice brought him back to the present.

"Yes, thanks, Grace. You've been really helpful."

"You know I can get into a lot of trouble for this, don't you? Bank records are supposed to be confidential."

"I know a good lawyer," he replied.

"Just keep me out of it."

He snapped his notebook shut. "Understood."

"See you at the party."

"Yeah." He disconnected the call and lay back on his bed. He should've been elated. His plan was so close to success. Instead, he felt oddly hollow. Picking up the photo of Analise that he'd taken from his sister's bedroom, he stared at her beautiful face. The picture was ten years old, yet Analise's incredible eyes were still the same. Eyes that had seen the worst of the world. He wanted to show her the best.

Still, what he'd come to Manitoba to do was almost complete. The man who had seduced his sister and then so publicly denounced her, pushing her to suicide, was on the verge of bankruptcy. Erik had carefully engineered Ian MacEwan's downfall. Ian was about to get his just desserts.

It had taken him two years and countless rounds of beer to eventually loosen tongues and uncover the truth about Karen's last days. It seemed the high school jocks had a pact to see how many girls they could bed before graduation. Analise had been their ultimate target. When she hadn't shown up for the final year-end party, Ian had decided that her best friend, Karen, would do.

The next day, when Karen, thinking they were now a couple, sat next to Ian in the cafeteria, he had told the truth. In fact, Ian had said, if he hadn't been so drunk, he would never have been able to stomach banging her. Humiliated and heartbroken, Karen had raced home after school, refusing to talk to anyone. Then Analise had found her best friend's body in the barn. And all their lives had been broken.

Grabbing his phone and wallet from the dresser, Erik left the room. His mother called out as he opened the screen door.

"Where are you going, Erik?"

"To see Analise. Don't wait up." After yesterday, he didn't have the patience to deal with his mother. He found her constant clinging almost unbearable. No wonder Analise steered clear of her as much as possible.

"It's only ten in the morning. Are you planning on staying away all day?"

"I'm not sure. I'll call you if I won't be home tonight." Before he could close the driver's door, his mother was there.

"I thought we could spend the day together," she said. He could already smell alcohol on her breath. He'd tried to hide it all, but obviously she had a secret stash.

If only she would recognize she had a problem and seek treatment. Until then, there wasn't a lot he could do to help her. He forced his voice to remain gentle. "We spent the whole day together yesterday. You kept me so busy cleaning up after the party, I didn't get to see my fiancée." And missing Analise had become a physical pain. Which didn't bode well for when they parted. *If* they parted, his heart amended. Damn optimistic heart.

"I haven't seen my son in a year and a half. I think the least you can do is spend some time with me." His mother's whining grated on his already taut nerves. He'd done his best to be patient, slipping her glasses of water between drinks. He needed a break.

"I love Analise. I want to be with her. I'll try to convince her to come over here." Although he doubted Analise would want to spend much time at the farm. There were too many memories of Karen tied up here. After her revelations about her fiancé's death, Erik wanted to remind her of life's joys, not its sorrows.

"If that's the best you can offer, I guess that will have to do."

Was there some way he could make his mother focus less on the past and try to find some joy in the future? A grandchild would probably do the trick. Wasn't that a scary thought.

His foul mood lifted as he parked in front of the Thordarsons' house. A day with Analise held endless opportunities to touch and kiss her, something he was finding more and more addictive. As he stepped from the BMW, Analise and her grandfather appeared on the porch. She wore a light blue skirt and white top, her handbag slung over her shoulder as though they were going out.

"Oh, Erik." She seemed surprised to see him, recovering quickly as her grandfather shot her a questioning glance. "*Afi* and I are leaving for Winnipeg. I should have called you—sorry you've had a wasted trip."

"Seeing you is never a wasted trip. And I've got nothing on today. Why don't I go with you to the city?"

"If Erik goes with you, then you don't need me," Gunnar said.

"But *Afi*, I want to spend more time with you." Analise put a hand on her grandfather's arm.

Erik winced at the contrast between Analise wanting to be with her family and him trying to avoid his.

"We were together all day yesterday. Go with Erik. I'm not feeling up to a long drive anyway."

Analise looked ready to argue. She put her bag down on the porch as her grandfather sat on the nearest rocking chair. Mounting the stairs in one bound, Erik caught hold of her hand. Raising it to his lips, he kissed each of her knuckles, holding her gaze as he lingered on the ring finger adorned with his diamond.

"We don't have to go today. We can stay home," she said. Her voice was breathless.

"I don't mind. I'm just happy to be with you," he said. The porch had been swept clean, the windows washed, and the tall grass around the house had been cut back. Two cans of paint sat by the door. They had been busy yesterday. Analise looked tired. He could help Gunnar paint while she supervised. Or both Thordarsons could sit on the porch and tell him what to do. "Is there something around here I could help with? I'm pretty handy with fences." Did she remember how he'd come over and help her grandfather when she was a teenager? Then, he'd made a big show of taking his shirt off and flexing his muscles, such as they were. It had worked to get her interest then, maybe it would help now.

For the first time, Gunnar looked at him with something like approval. "Go, sweet. Spend the day with Erik. You don't need an old man tagging along."

"*Afi*, you're not an old man," she protested.

"And I'm not going anywhere. I'll still be here when you get back," her granddad encouraged.

With a defeated sigh, she kissed her grandfather's cheek, picked up her handbag, and followed Erik off the steps.

"Your vehicle or mine?" She jangled her keys.

"We can take yours. Why don't you drive into town, and I'll drive back?"

"Really?" Unlocking the doors, she slipped behind the steering wheel. "Jean-Claude never let me drive. He always had to be in control," she added as she pulled onto the main road.

"I'm *not* Jean-Claude." He cared less about control than the opportunity to spend the next hour and a half looking at the beautiful woman next to him.

"Yes, I'm beginning to realize."

As they approached the city, Erik noticed she fiddled with her sunglasses and her left leg bounced up and down to a rapid, silent rhythm. The drive in had been pleasant enough. They'd discussed her favorite places in the world and where she'd avoid in the future. She'd also quizzed him on the merger he'd been working on, seeming to be interested in the process most people found boring in the extreme.

"What did you want to do in Winnipeg?"

"I need to pick up a few things. I didn't pack for such a long stay. Plus, with all the events surrounding your grandparents' anniversary, I need a dress or two. How fancy is the big celebration?" Her smile was tight.

"It'll be pretty formal. The women in my family will take any opportunity to break out their party dresses." He salivated at the thought of previewing Analise in a dozen formal dresses. He envisaged low cleavage and lots of gorgeous leg. Shopping had never held such appeal.

Taking the ring road, she drove to Polo Park mall, pulling into a stall near The Bay store. She handed Erik the keys.

"Clothes shopping will probably bore you to tears.

Why don't you take the car, and I'll meet you back here in a couple of hours?" she suggested as she exited the vehicle.

"No, I'm good. I'll come with you. I'm looking forward to selecting dresses for you to try on."

Analise put her hand on her hip. "I'm not a doll to be dressed for your pleasure. I shop alone."

He was about to argue, then remembered her former fiancé's control issues. "All right. But we haven't celebrated our engagement. Will you let me take you for dinner after you're done?"

"You want to celebrate a fake engagement?"

He caressed the back of her neck before he lowered his mouth to hers. "If it were a real engagement, we'd have partied naked with a bottle of champagne, a bowl of strawberries, and some whipped cream," he whispered against her lips.

She stepped back, breaking the contact. "Dinner it is, then. I'll text you when I'm done, and you can tell me where to meet you."

Wandering around the city alone was not the way he wanted to spend the day. But he was playing the long game. A strategic retreat now could mean a proper celebration later. "I'll book a table at the Palm Room Lounge at Hotel Fort Garry. And I'll get a room if you want to take a nap or change before dinner."

"Hotel Fort Garry? You don't do things cheap, Prairie Boy."

"Not for my best fiancée."

"You got a second-class one stashed somewhere?"

"Nope. You're all the woman I need."

"We'll see." She turned on her heel and walked away without a backward glance.

He locked his knees to stop from following her. He sensed there was something more than the deaths of her fiancé and grandmother bothering her. Was she preparing to run away again? Because he sure as hell wasn't ready to say good-bye.

***

Analise dragged her weary body into the iconic Winnipeg hotel. She dropped her shopping bags in front of the reception desk.

"My, uh … Erik Sigurdson said he booked a room here."

"You must be Miss Thordarson. Mr. Sigurdson has a room for you, and he's left a note," the receptionist said.

Analise signed the registration document and then picked up the envelope.

My darling Analise,

I hope your shopping trip was successful. If you make it to the hotel in time, please feel free to pamper yourself in the spa. Nothing will be able to make you more beautiful, but perhaps you might enjoy a massage or facial. I'll meet you at the restaurant at 7 p.m. But if you need more time, just call my cell.

Your loving fiancé,
Prairie Boy

Maybe a little pampering was what she needed—to let go of the stress and worry for a few hours and recapture her peace. Which would evaporate the second she saw Erik and her body clamored for what it couldn't have. She passed her bags to the concierge and headed to the spa.

Analise fell asleep during her massage and facial. When she woke, her makeup had also been done. A coat of mascara was all that was needed to complete the transformation. She felt a million times better. More like the real Analise, not the tired-out, injured shell of a woman who'd slumped into town a few days ago. She was ready to take on the world. Or at least the Erik-inhabited portion of it.

Didn't they say the way to get over one man was to get under another? Although, that had the potential to end in even greater disaster. And there were few places left for her to run. Anywhere in Africa or the Middle East was out of the question; the French government was still investigating whether she was involved in her former fiancé's activities, so her passport was undoubtedly flagged.

At least having pawned Jean-Claude's engagement ring, she now was semi-solvent. But the pawn shop had only been able to give her a fraction of its worth, so she was nowhere near being able to pay off Erik. Which meant she'd have to stick around, at least until her name was cleared. She was still debating whether to tell Erik the full story and ask for his help or not.

She pushed open the door to the room Erik had

booked and smiled. Prairie Boy didn't do things by half. It was more than a room—she stepped into a luxury suite. She kicked off her shoes and let her toes sink into the soft carpet. She had less than half an hour, though, to dress for dinner, so she went in search of her shopping bags. Hopefully, one of the dresses she'd bought would be suitable for the fancy restaurant.

Spread out on the bed was a beautiful designer dress, together with some wispy underwear and the most gorgeous pair of black Louboutin shoes she'd seen. Having lived in combat boots for the past four years, she'd never had much of a shoe fetish, but these babies were enough to make her start one.

Despite telling herself a hundred times that she wasn't going to fall in with whatever nefarious scheme Erik had planned, she put on the dress and slipped on the shoes. She did a twirl and then glanced in the mirror. Not bad. The heels gave her some height, and the dress showed off her curves to the best advantage. She felt like a woman again.

Except her stomach was as full of butterflies as if she were going on her first date. Did he expect that after celebrating their fake engagement with dinner they'd move on to the champagne, strawberries, and whipped cream festivities?

Would she object if he did?

She still hadn't decided when she approached the entrance to the Palm Room Lounge. Wearing a whisper of red silk and chiffon, teetering on a pair of stilettos, she was overdressed and underdressed at the same time.

Before she could spy Erik in the darkened interior, he appeared at her side. He'd changed into a dark suit, a crisp white shirt, and a bright red tie that matched her dress. She hadn't thought he could look better than in fitted jeans and a T-shirt. She'd been wrong.

"You are stunning," he whispered into her ear as he led her to a quiet table tucked against the far wall. He brushed a kiss against her temple as he pushed in her chair. Damn, the man smelled good, too.

"I thought I told you I wasn't a doll, Prairie Boy," she said as he sat opposite her. Unfortunately, the breathiness of her voice turned the rebuke into more of a sexy come-on, making it sound like she wasn't to be dressed but rather undressed.

"And yet you put it on?" He ignored her glare and ran his index finger over the knuckles of her clenched fist.

"I guess there's a woman in me somewhere who still likes pretty things." She shrugged, trying to ignore the soft caress of the material against her skin. And Erik's one finger that was wreaking havoc with her control.

"You're all woman, Analise. Don't let anyone tell you otherwise. A strong, beautiful woman." The heat of his gaze set off warm tingles over her exposed skin. Mesmerized by his eyes, she didn't notice the waiter had appeared beside the table until he spoke.

"May I take your drinks order?"

Forcing herself to look away from Erik, she gave the waiter a small smile. "Just an orange juice for me."

"We're celebrating—wouldn't you rather have

champagne?" Erik asked.

"I'll stick with the juice." Her mother's dependence on drink and drugs had made Analise wary of any predisposition to substance abuse. Although, her father's constant infidelity probably had more to do with her mother's downfall than any inheritable tendency. Plus, she was having enough difficulty staying in control of her body without alcohol reducing her inhibitions.

Erik ordered a glass of wine, then leaned forward again. He ran his fingers up her arm to her elbow and back down again. His touch was smoother and more potent than eighteen-year-old Scotch. They spoke of favorite foods, her photography, and his love of sailing. At some point they transitioned to the restaurant. Erik's arm around her waist held her tightly against him. Anyone watching them would have no doubts that they were a couple in love. Analise herself was having trouble remembering it was all a façade.

As the waiter cleared their dinner plates, Analise excused herself to use the ladies' room. As she washed her hands, she stared in the mirror, hardly able to believe the image that reflected back. She glowed. The dark circles under her eyes had disappeared. Her cheeks were flushed, and she couldn't even blame a glass of wine. Excitement hummed through her body and, in the spirit of honesty, a drum of desire also pounded in her veins. Erik was gorgeous, and all evening he'd gazed on her with undisguised lust, tempered with a hint of reverence and care. If only she could erase the past ten years. Go back to the sweet, innocent girl who still believed in happy-ever-afters.

As she exited, she spotted a pay phone tucked in the corner of the hallway. Just her luck. She'd been searching all day, and she'd finally found one when Erik was only meters away. But it was the closest she was likely to get to untraceable private communication. With no time to waste, she dug into the bottom of her purse and pulled out the huge bag of coins she'd prepared for just such an eventuality. As she slotted the money into the phone, she carefully extracted the delicate paper with the number written in Jean-Claude's nearly illegible Arabic scrawl.

She glanced around, praying that Erik didn't also make a trip to the washroom. Her fingers shook as she punched in the numbers. An eternity passed before she heard the distant ring through the earpiece. Hopefully, the connection would be decent, and she wouldn't need to shout.

"*Oui.*" The call was answered on the second ring by a male voice speaking French.

"*Je m'appelle—*"

"I know who you are." The caller switched to English. "He is dead?"

"Yes."

"Buy a cheap cell phone with cash. Text this number with the GPS coordinates of a location exactly ten days before you are able to meet. Then dispose of the phone somewhere it will never be found." The voice was harsh and spoke with an Arab accent.

"How will I know you?"

"I will find you. Choose a place very public. Tell

no one."

The line went dead before she could ask another question.

"Analise?"

She turned to find Erik striding toward her. Replacing the receiver, she gave herself a mental shake.

Tell no one.

"I wanted to call my granddad and let him know I'm okay. He probably expected us back before now."

"Why didn't you say something? I'd have loaned you my cell. Don't you have one?"

"The battery's dead. I keep forgetting to charge it," she prevaricated.

"Did you get through?"

"What? Oh, um, no. I must have misdialed. The number is on speed dial on my cell phone; I guess I remembered it wrong."

"Here." Erik handed her his phone. "The number's in my contacts under 'Thordarson.'" He pushed open the door of the men's room and disappeared inside.

Analise scrolled through the names on Erik's phone, trying not to notice the number of women's names. She had no claim on him. Unfortunately, that didn't lessen the burning sensation in her chest. Finding her grandfather's number, she pressed the call button.

Should she tell *Afi* that she'd be back later tonight or not until tomorrow? Was this the date she and Erik had missed all those years ago? The one with the secret plan to spend the night together?

Chapter Seven

Erik returned to the table, and Analise rose majestically as he neared. As soon as he'd seen the dress in the store window, he knew she'd look fabulous in it. She deserved to be wrapped in silk and treasured, not treated like a disposable plaything as her previous fiancé had done. Ever since Analise had told him about Jean-Claude, the need to protect and cherish her had become almost overwhelming.

He'd already paid the bill, assuming she didn't want dessert because she hadn't finished her meal. If she did, they could always order room service. Protecting and cherishing weren't the only needs that hummed through his body.

"Did you talk to your granddad?" Erik wrapped his arms around her. God, she felt as good as she looked. The top of her head fit perfectly under his chin. Her soft curves touched in all the right places. Ten years seemed to have intensified rather than dulled the longing.

"Yes. He said as long as I'm with you, he's not worried."

"Are you worried?"

"No. I'm a big girl. I can look after myself."

What did she mean by that? "Let's go up to the room to collect your things." Like being alone with her was going to help calm his libido.

"I do need to change before we go home," she replied.

Was she unaware of the sexual tension between them? He might need a cold shower while she changed. Then her gaze roved over his lips, and she licked her own. His mouth went dry.

The *bing* of the elevator arriving at their floor was like a timer going off in his body. *Ready*.

He opened the suite door and let her precede him. His gaze lingered on her tight backside hugged by the red silk fabric. God, this so wasn't helping.

She turned as he closed the door, her eyes uncertain as he stepped toward her. He stopped. His own breathing became shallow.

"Analise?" He wanted to make sure she was on the same page.

He waited while myriad emotions flickered across her face: loneliness, longing, lust. She walked over to the desk, her fingers toying with the pen on the notepad. Erik released a slow breath to calm his racing heart.

"If you want to change before we go, I'll wait here." He offered her an easy exit.

"No, I…" Her voice was husky. She seemed unable to move but held her hand out to him.

Crossing the room in three strides, he framed her face with his hands. He searched her eyes, needing to know if she was sure. She blinked, then parted her lips. Before his brain finished analyzing the answer in her eyes, her body was plastered against his and he was plundering her mouth like a hormonal teenager. Wanting to take things slow, in case she changed her mind, he eased back, only to have her hand thread through his hair and pull his mouth back to hers. Her other hand rested against his chest, hopefully holding in his heart as it banged against his rib cage.

As much as he wanted to stay there and kiss her for a full hour, their height difference was giving him a neck ache. So he lifted her and strode over to the sofa. He sat with Analise in his lap, her slight weight pressing against his arousal. A groan escaped his lips as she wiggled. Her breathing was rapid, her lips swollen from his kisses. The strap of her dress slid down her arm, revealing another centimeter of breast. He traced the line of her cleavage with his index finger, watching her eyes as they darkened.

Her hips shimmied again, and Erik clenched his teeth to stop himself from rocketing her off him. This wasn't going to work. Neither of them was in control. Any other time in their relationship, it would've been the ideal situation. He'd never experienced such explosive passion before. But this was their first time; no way was he going to rush it.

With a swift move he laid her on the sofa while he kneeled on the floor. She was spread out before him like an all-you-can-eat buffet, and he intended to gorge himself. Her breasts rose and fell rapidly, and he forced his eyes to look away. That was dessert. Stripping off his suit jacket and tie, he set to play. He moved down to her feet and slid off her shoes. Raising her foot, he feathered kisses along her delicate ankle, repeating the slow torment with her other foot.

He traced his lips from her inner ankle up to her knee, his fingers exploring ahead. She gasped and writhed beneath him as he hit the barrier of her underwear. Slowly, he retreated until he was back at her ankles again. He performed the same operation with her other leg. As he reached her upper thigh, his name escaped her lips. He raised his head at that; her eyes were tightly closed, and her head thrashed from side to side on the pillow. A surge of pure masculine pride flowed through him, giving him the necessary restraint to make this good for her before he satisfied his own needs.

Her hand was clenched on the side of the sofa, pulling on the upholstery. Erik pried her fingers off the furniture and kissed each digit until her hand went limp in his. He then trailed his lips around her wrist, his tongue pressing against her pulse. Her inner elbow received a similar treatment, and by the time he reached her shoulder, she was moaning with pleasure. Tracing the line of her cleavage with his finger again, his thumb rested on her nipple. Analise arched her back, and his other hand lowered the zipper on her dress. All that remained was to lift off the fabric and feast his senses.

Placing his index finger at the top of her dress, he slid it down, revealing, millimeter by millimeter, her glorious, white flesh. At the first hint of a darker color he stopped, waiting for her eyes to open. When they did, he leaned down and kissed her parted lips.

Her hands raced up and down his back, tugging at the fabric of his shirt. He sat up so she could undo the buttons, memorizing her face flushed with passion. Her white teeth bit into her bottom lip as she concentrated on her task. Wanting to test her control, he circled his thumbs over her nipples through the bunched fabric of her dress. Analise gave up on the last two buttons and ripped the shirt the rest of the way open. Her hands ran over his chest and abs, and it was his turn to moan.

"May I?" He had the fabric of her dress between finger and thumb, holding it a centimeter away from her body before lowering it again to caress her taut peaks and lifting it off again.

"Please—" she gasped.

"Oh, I intend to," he replied. He pulled the material down to her waist and let his eyes feast on the bounty before him. "You are exquisite."

Before he could say anything further, Analise threaded her fingers through his hair and pulled his head down to her breast. He circled the peak with his tongue before taking it into his mouth. His own body was harder than a steel beam. He clamped down on his desire. Ensuring Analise enjoyed the moment was his first priority.

He switched over to her other breast, his fingers replacing his lips on the first, plucking then circling and caressing in time with his tongue. Lifting his gaze, he saw her head again roll back and forth on the cushion, a soft mewling coming from her parted lips. With his free hand he reached down to her ankle, his fingers and thumb tracing lazy circles up to her inner thigh. He slipped his hand around to cup her bottom, massaging her clenched muscles. Sliding his hand down the outside of her thigh, he intended to repeat the movement when his palm encountered a large, raised welt. Analise flinched, and a moan of pain, not passion, escaped her lips.

A shiver coursed through Erik that had nothing to do with desire.

***

Analise's eyes flew open. A cool draft blew over her flushed skin as Erik moved away. He switched from consummate lover to clinician in a heartbeat.

"What's that?" he asked.

Flipping on the light at the end of the sofa, he turned her leg to see the injury. She pulled the top of her dress back in place and sat up on her elbows.

"It's only a scratch." Desire drummed through her veins. The heat of Erik's loving had been so intense, her insides had melted and her brain had fogged over.

"That's more than a scratch. And it's recent. When did you get it?" The pad of Erik's thumb traced gently around the injury, careful not to touch it again.

She pulled her leg out of his hand and sat up. Slipping her arms through the straps, she managed to pull the zipper back up on her dress without dislocating her shoulder.

"A souvenir of Syria."

"I thought you said you evaded the soldiers." Erik picked up his suit jacket from the floor and put it around her shoulders, then he pulled her back to rest against his naked chest. His heartbeat had lessened to a rhythmic thud, although his breathing was still faster than normal.

"After Jean-Claude died, I went to find help to move his body. I couldn't leave him there; he deserved a decent burial. As I exited the building there was an explosion across the road. Next thing I knew I woke up in a hospital bed." *A hospital in Algeria, not Syria, but as I have no idea how I got there, it's probably not relevant.*

"And that was your only injury?"

"You just did a pretty thorough physical." She crossed her arms, giving herself a hug to ward off the chill of his rejection.

"Analise…" Erik put his finger under her chin and raised her face to his. "I'm sorry."

Sorry for my injury? Sorry that you started to make love to me? Or sorry that you stopped?

"It doesn't matter. It's past." She pulled out of his arms. "I'll change, then I want to go home." *Dieu,* she was an idiot. She'd let the past lull her into thinking this was her future. Their engagement was fake, and she needed to remember that. Just because she wanted him didn't mean she should have him. Even though it had been … amazing.

Gaining the sanctity of the bedroom, Analise collapsed on the bed.

Amazing, but too soon.

She'd only given Erik the censored version of events. When she'd begged Jean-Claude not to go off to meet his source, his response was to make love to her. She thought he'd changed his mind, that he'd stay.

But after the final orgasmic spasms had wracked her body, he'd pulled his pants back on and sauntered out the door, blowing her a kiss as he stepped through. Next time she'd seen him, death was in his eyes.

She didn't want to use Erik to forget Jean-Claude. If she slept with Erik, it had to be because she loved him, not just for some physical release. It had to mean something.

Analise yanked off the dress, not caring if she tore the expensive fabric. She pulled on her T-shirt and skirt and stuffed her feet into her ballerina flats. Shoving the dress into the plastic laundry bag, she left the room.

Erik stood next to the window, his shirt still undone. He was disheveled and delectable, and for a microsecond she thought about staying.

"I'll wait in the lobby," she said as she strode toward the door. She didn't turn back and blow him a kiss.

Chapter Eight

Erik pulled up once again in front of the Thordarson house. He'd dropped Analise off at two in the morning the preceding day. She hadn't said a word the whole trip back from Winnipeg and had just whispered, "*Bonne nuit*," as she'd slammed the car door shut. Then, yesterday, she'd refused his calls. Her grandfather claimed she was *resting*.

The only good thing to come out of the past twenty-four hours was that his mother had managed to stay sober the entire time. He could've used a drink. He'd made a real mess of things in Winnipeg. Instead of protecting and cherishing Analise, he was using and abusing, just like her former fiancé. After their fake engagement was over, she'd leave again. He had no right to make love to her.

However, there were still ten days to go until his grandparents' anniversary. Unless he wanted to answer some very uncomfortable inquiries from his family in the coming days, he'd have to make up to her somehow. Question was, where to start?

As he stepped from the BMW, he noticed a few more changes to the Thordarson homestead. There were now two baskets of flowers on the railing, and the door had been painted. The screen door opened as he stepped onto the porch, and Analise stood before him.

Her hands were on her hips, her shoulders back, her chin raised, ready to do battle. Despite all that life had thrown at her, she wasn't cowering in the corner. She was ready to take on the world. Her fierce determination, tempered by a caring heart, took his breath away.

The summer dress she wore had small buttons all the way from the neckline to the hem. Dear God, what he wouldn't give to undo every single one of those buttons and kiss each centimeter of skin as it was revealed.

To keep his hands off, he adjusted the ball cap on his head.

"Hi," he said as she stopped in front of him. A trickle of sweat that had nothing to do with the thirty-five-degree Celsius temperature ran down his back.

"What do you want, Erik?" Her voice was so cold he could almost see her breath in the air.

"To talk about what happened in Winnipeg. I'm sorry; I took advantage of you. I won't do it again." He'd obviously misread her signals. His own desire for her had clouded his judgment.

She shook her head, then leaned against the doorframe. "It's not that. I'm mad at myself more than you. I let myself get caught up in the romance and forgot this is all fake. Six weeks ago, I held my fiancé in my arms as he bled to death. Yes, our relationship was troubled and heading for the finish line. But that doesn't mean I should just jump into bed with the next guy who comes along."

"I'm not the next guy. I'm the original guy."

"Which makes it even more complicated. I look at you, and what I felt back then gets all muddled with what I feel now. I can't tell what's real anymore. And that frightens me."

It scared the shit out of him as well. But he wasn't about to give up. "Analise, I need you."

For a second, a light flared in her beautiful eyes, then it was gone. "I made a promise, and I don't go back on my word. I'll still pretend to be your loving fiancée when we're with your family. The rest of the time I want you to leave me alone." Her voice was weary, as though there was little fight left in her.

"I can't do that." The words were wrung from him.

"Why not?" Her aqua eyes appraised him, leaving him no choice but to tell her the truth.

"Because I can't stay away from you. I don't know whether it's our unresolved past, our convoluted present, or the lure of the future. All I know is that I want to spend every moment I can with you."

Her eyes searched his, but she didn't resist when he pulled her closer. He didn't dare risk a kiss so he simply held her against him until he felt her relax.

"This isn't surrender, Prairie Boy," she murmured against his chest.

"I'll settle for a truce."

"Okay, truce."

A sigh escaped her, and she melted into his embrace. The pressure in his chest eased a bit, and he was able to take a deep breath. Her subtle scent of lemons heated with cinnamon enveloped him.

"Come sailing with me," he said against the top of

her head.

"Sailing?" Analise pulled back to look him in the face.

"My cousin said we could use his boat. It's moored in Gimli Harbour."

"I don't know. I was going to spend the day working on the house with *Afi*."

"Go with Erik, sweet," Gunnar said as he came around the corner from the barn. "The house will still be here when you get back."

"I..." She was obviously searching for an excuse.

"You love sailing, or at least you used to," Gunnar added. "No point staying mad at your man for long. Go and enjoy your day."

Still, she hesitated.

"Come on, love. The sun is glorious, and there's just enough of a breeze for a nice sail." Erik tucked a strand of her hair behind her ear, lingering in the caress.

"Oh, all right. I'll get changed." She re-entered the house, her steps a little lighter than when she'd first come to the door.

"Sit down, son." Gunnar climbed onto the porch and indicated the rocking chair next to him.

Erik searched the other man's face. Was he about to be chewed out for upsetting Analise? He tried to marshal a contrite expression.

"I'm sorry I brought your granddaughter home so late the other night." He felt eighteen years old again. That was about the last time he'd had to justify his actions to a parental figure.

"That's not what I want to talk to you about.

Analise told me you paid off my debts."

Erik took a deep breath. He'd known this conversation would come eventually, and he still had no idea how to handle it. If he was across a boardroom table, it would be no problem, just another business transaction. But here? He could hardly say he did it to get Analise to pretend to be his fiancée. "I couldn't let a neighbor go to the wall. You've had a bad couple of years. You can pay me back when you're on your feet again."

Gunnar looked out at the neglected yard and empty paddock and shook his head.

"I think it's time for the next generation to take over. Since Lara's passing, my heart isn't here anymore. I know you're a hotshot lawyer and Analise is all wrapped up in her photography. Do you think you'll settle in Manitoba after your wedding?"

Erik swallowed. *Damn it, where is Analise?* "We haven't made a decision yet. I'm still under contract with the law firm in London." And he'd been offered a partnership if he wanted to stay in the United Kingdom. He'd be at the top of his career ladder, able to pick and choose his clients and assignments.

"Well, I'm gonna put the property in your names anyway. You can always decide what to do with it when you make your minds up." The older man's shoulders slumped.

"There's no need, Mr. Thordarson. Keep it in your name for now, or change it to Analise only."

"Why? You changing your mind about marrying my granddaughter?" Gunnar stopped rocking and stared at Erik.

"No," he quickly interjected. "But this is your land and her inheritance. Once we're married, we can change things over to joint tenancy."

"When are you getting married? I know it's fashionable these days to have long engagements, but I don't hold with that. I'd have wed Lara the next day if I could. Course, back then, we waited to consummate the relationship until after the vows were taken."

Erik's face flamed. He was saved from answering by Analise's reappearance, a small camera bag slung over her shoulder.

"*Afi*, I told you, Erik and I will set a date in a few months' time. We just got engaged and still have a lot of issues to discuss, such as where we'll live. When we do make wedding arrangements, you'll be the first to know." She stooped and kissed her grandfather on the cheek.

"I'm just looking out for you, sweet. You've got no one else to do it."

"She's got me now," Erik corrected.

Gunnar nodded. "Well, enjoy your sail. Keep an eye on the weather, though. This hot streak has got to break soon, and when it does, it'll be a doozy of a storm."

"We will," Erik answered. As Analise got comfortable in the passenger seat, he checked out her new outfit. She'd changed into a long pair of shorts, a faded, striped top, and a pair of lace-up sneakers. She rocked the sexy, casual look.

"Top up or down?" His finger hovered over the

button to retract the car's roof.

"Down. It's a lovely day, might as well enjoy it. As *Afi* said, it's going to end sometime."

Was she still talking about the weather?

Erik pulled onto the main road leading to the nearby lakeside community. He glanced over at Analise as she stared at the passing scenery. Her shorts had ridden up, and the welt on her leg was visible below the hem.

"Does it still hurt?" He ran a finger around the injury. Her skin quivered under his touch.

"Not as much anymore. And I finished the antibiotics yesterday. They were making me feel queasy."

"I'm glad." When it didn't seem as though she was going to add to the conversation, he searched for another topic. "So, what did you do yesterday? Did you really rest like your grandfather said?"

"A little. I slept till ten and had a lazy morning. Then we went to my grandmother's grave again and planted some flowers. When we got back we tidied the house and yard a bit, and then I had another sleep. I don't know why I'm so tired. I usually adjust to time zones quicker than this."

"You've not only been injured but also experienced emotional trauma. Your body is probably just telling you to take it easy for a while."

"I guess. So how big is your cousin's boat? I haven't sailed for years, so I don't think I'll be much good at helping out."

"It's only a little one, twenty feet. I can handle it

on my own. You just need to relax, maybe hold the tiller for a few minutes while I get the sails sorted. My dad had a boat when we were growing up. I've spent quite a bit of time on the water, so you don't have to worry that we'll sink. If you start to feel ill or want to go home, let me know."

"Thanks. I went out on your dad's boat once with Karen. I loved it, but she was sick the whole time so we never went again."

"Karen was the same as my mom—neither enjoyed the boat. I'd have taken you out sailing if you'd have told me."

Analise raised an eyebrow. Yeah, he was having enough trouble keeping his hands off her now. Ten years ago, there'd have been no chance, with just the two of them on his father's boat, alone in the middle of the lake.

Twenty minutes later, they were aboard and headed out of the harbor. The wind blew gently through her hair, ruffling the ends. She stretched her legs out as she leaned back, raising her face to the sunshine. A flood of warmth rushed through him.

After clearing the last navigation buoy, Erik slowed the engine and pointed the boat into the wind.

"Can you hold the tiller while I get the sails up?"

Analise scooted along the seat and took the wooden handle, her hand skimming his. This time, it was his skin that quivered at the touch. Sails hoisted, Erik relieved Analise of the helm. "My gran packed a picnic lunch for us if you're hungry. It's in the green backpack."

She ducked into the cabin and retrieved the bag while he enjoyed the view of her superfine ass. These solo dates were murder on the self-control. Problem was, even when they were around others, the only thing he could think of was getting her alone.

"How long did your gran think we were going for? There's enough food here for a week." Analise pulled out several sealed containers of salads, sandwiches, raw vegetables, pasta, and one with chicken drumsticks.

"She's Ukrainian. Food is their thing. You can never eat enough to satisfy a Ukrainian baba."

"Do you want me to dish up something for you?"

"Naw, just hand me one of those chicken legs and save me some salad."

After a few minutes' silence as they both devoured the tasty chicken, Analise looked him in the eye.

"Why did you have an engagement ring in your pocket the first day we met again?"

He tossed the chicken bone into the water and wiped his hands on the napkin she'd wrapped around the leg. "I had a girlfriend, a fellow lawyer. Brenda and I worked for the same law firm in Toronto. When the largest client launched a takeover bid for its Britain-based rival, we were asked to go to London and act as counsel during the merger negotiations. We worked very closely together, and late dinners turned into overnights, and soon we were pretty much living in each other's pockets. She started hinting that after a year together it was time to take the relationship to the next level. That, plus the constant nagging from my mother about getting married, put ideas in my head.

One day, I was walking by a jeweler's, saw the ring, and bought it."

Even to his ears it sounded cold and calculated. But Brenda had seemed the perfect lawyer's wife, especially if he took the partnership. She'd loved London—the shopping, weekends in Paris or Milan, the status of being wife to a partner in one of Britain's top law firms. As he thought back, it struck him that Brenda had begun to hint about marriage shortly after he'd told her about the partnership offer.

His gaze roved over Analise as she popped a cherry tomato into her mouth. She grabbed her camera out of the cabin and took a few photos of a pair of ducks swimming near the boat. As they drew alongside, the ducks took to flight, the sunlight glinting off the colorful feathers of the male. This was where she belonged, out in nature, capturing its beauty. Not in a war zone, dodging snipers.

But not in London, either. He couldn't imagine her enjoying London life, attending boring dinners with his fellow lawyers or fundraising with the other partners' wives. And he couldn't imagine sleeping alone while he waited for her to return from some distant photography assignment, wondering if she was safe. Analise had her own world, and he wasn't part of it.

He couldn't imagine life with her—or without her.

"Sounds like you and Brenda had a lot in common." Her voice was soft, almost sad.

"Not really. Once the merger wrapped up we found we had nothing to talk about. We came back to Toronto on holiday and stayed with her family for a week. And we were so bored with each other. I never worked up the nerve to give her the ring, so it sat in my pocket until I gave it to you." They weren't even really engaged and he couldn't contemplate asking Analise to return his ring.

"Um, is she still in Toronto waiting for you to come back and propose? What if she shows up here to surprise you? That'll make your grandparents' party memorable."

It was the first time in days he'd seen that mischievous twinkle in her eyes. His laugh boomed out across the water, causing a flock of pelicans to divert their flight path.

"I'm pretty sure she won't turn up. I told her I thought we needed a break, and she seemed almost relieved. I haven't heard from her in two weeks. In fact, I haven't even thought about her since I saw you again. It's definitely over. How can I marry a woman I don't even miss?" Unlike yesterday, when he'd checked his phone every five minutes, hoping Analise would message him to come around.

Analise nodded. "Have you had enough?"

"What?" He was starting to suspect there wasn't anything about Analise he'd ever have enough of. She gestured at the containers of food. "Oh, yeah, thanks."

Analise packed up the food and returned the backpack to the cabin, also storing her camera. "Okay if I go up front and sunbathe for a while?"

Erik swallowed. *Hell, yeah!* "If you need me to put cream anywhere, let me know," he offered.

Once up front, she peeled off her t-shirt and shorts,

revealing a navy blue bikini. Fortunately, the mast and angle of the cabin hid most of her lithe body from his view. What he did see was enough to raise his temperature. The light had been dim at the hotel, and he'd been concentrating on each delectable bit of her. Seeing the whole package in the bright light of day was almost too much to resist.

But resist he must. After what happened in Winnipeg, he needed to let her make the first move.

To take his mind off the scantily clad Analise feet away from him, he concentrated on his main objective in returning to Manitoba: Ian MacEwan's downfall. Ian's final hope had been to buy the failing Thordarson stables. Now that Erik had paid off the bank, that option was gone. All that remained was to call in all the demand loans he had provided to Ian under the guise of development and start-up financing through shadow companies. Then, Ian would have no option but to sell his home and land and start over.

At least he'd get a second chance. Karen hadn't.

But would ruining Ian really bring anyone any happiness? What would his grandparents say when they discovered he'd deliberately destroyed another man's livelihood? His stomach roiled. People in the prairies stuck together. It was the only way to survive.

A sudden gust of wind snapped the sail to the other side. If he hadn't ducked, he'd have been knocked overboard by the boom. Analise sat up, grabbing for the mast as the boat heeled over.

"Everything all right?" she called out.

Erik glanced at the sky. A menacing black cloud

loomed on the horizon, growing larger each second he stared at it. "I think that storm your granddad mentioned might be coming in. Can you take the helm while I get the engine started and pull the sails down?"

"You don't think it'll just pass over?" She sheltered her eyes with one hand while holding the mast with the other.

"I'm not going to take the chance. We'll head back to the harbor. We can always shelter at Arnes if it hits before we get back to Gimli."

As she reached over to grab her shirt and shorts the boat lurched again, causing the clothes to fall into the water. Analise would have tumbled in herself if she hadn't grabbed on to one of the stays securing the mast.

"Are you okay?" His heart leapt into his throat as she scrambled back to the cockpit, holding the guardrail rope as she went.

"Fine. Be careful," she cautioned, as he leaned over the back and the boat lurched again. She held the tiller with both hands as he pulled on the starter cord for the engine. After several stutters, the little motor roared to life.

"Okay, try to hold her bow into the wind while I wrap the sails."

Erik secured the boat and returned to take the helm. Clouds now masked the sun, and with only her bikini on, she shivered. He pulled off his shirt and handed it to her.

"The storm is coming real fast. Do you think we'll make it back in time?"

He reached out and turned the little motor up to its

highest speed. "We might catch the edge of it, but I think we'll be safely in harbor before the real force hits. I'm sorry; I should have been keeping a better eye on the sky, especially after your granddad's warning."

"Well, I'm not made of sugar, so I won't melt. Actually, I'm impressed you're heading for shore at all. Jean-Claude would have wanted to test his strength against the power of Mother Nature." Her gaze swept once more over his chest before refocusing on the darkened horizon.

"I'll say it again: I'm not your former fiancé. I will never take a chance with your life."

"What about my heart?" The words were spoken so low, and with the frantic flapping of the sail edge in the wind, he wasn't sure she'd actually spoken. Not until her pain-filled eyes met his.

"Come, sit beside me." She sat stiffly next to him on the fiberglass bench, and he wrapped his free arm around her shoulders. "Analise, I know we have an unresolved relationship, and I will admit that seeing you again has brought all those feelings back. But we're different people now. I'm not sure I can offer you a future that you want. And as much as I crave your body, I realize that you've been through a very difficult few months. I don't want you to confuse blinding passion with a promise I can't make."

"You're right, I know. My life has changed so much in the past six weeks that I don't even know who I am anymore." She collapsed against him like a puppet whose strings had suddenly been released.

"You're   Analise   Thordarson,   beloved

granddaughter, fabulous woman, wonderful photographer, and current fake fiancée of one pig-headed, self-centered, carnally obsessed lawyer."

A small smile creased her full lips. "Have you ever wondered how our lives would have been different if Karen hadn't…" The smile disappeared.

He tucked her closer against his chest as a shudder wracked her body. "Every day."

***

Analise was soaked through, and although she was doing her very best to hold back the shivers, her body shook like she was holding a live power line. Huddled in the cabin, wearing her bikini and Erik's T-shirt, she found an old towel wedged between the seat cushions and wrapped it around her legs.

At least she didn't have to worry about disposing of the cheap cell phone she'd bought with her granddad the day before. It had been in the pocket of the shorts that had gone overboard. She'd texted the coordinates for a meeting while Erik had been getting the boat ready. Now, she wished she could discuss it with Erik, but the voice on the phone had warned her to tell no one. If she told Erik, he'd insist on coming with her. Then, the person she was to meet might not approach if she weren't alone. *Merde,* what a mess.

Through the cabin doorway she could see Erik tying the line at the rear of the boat to the dock. Rain poured off his naked back, and his shorts were plastered to his ass, emphasizing the curve of his butt.

A flicker of warmth flowed through her. Make that a surge of heat. As she watched, he ran his hand over his face to clear it of water before glancing in the direction of the car park. A second later, he joined her in the cabin. The tiny space filled with large, hard man. *Mon Dieu.*

"I've got some bad news," he said. He picked up the Plexiglas section that formed part of the entranceway and slid it into place. He popped the lower bit of the door in as well, leaving a half-meter gap for airflow. At least it stopped the wind from howling in their ears.

"What?" she managed to get out between clenched teeth, trying to stop them from chattering.

"I forgot to put the roof up on the BMW, so the car is soaked as well. We can either huddle in here until the rain stops or sit in the wet car. At least I can put the heater on in there."

Through the tiny window, she could see the rain coming down almost sideways. The deafening clanging of ropes slapping against the bare masts of all the sailboats in the harbor added to the tension. Make a mad dash through the weather to sit in a sodden car, or huddle where they were in the relative dry? "I don't think this will last for long. I vote for staying here." At least in the boat they were private and didn't have to scramble to the car with everyone watching.

"I agree. You're freezing, though. This is going to sound really self-serving, but if you take off my shirt and we huddle together, our combined body heat should warm you."

She raised an eyebrow at him but pulled off the soaked shirt, shuddering as the cool air hit her bare skin. Erik stretched out on the long bench that ran under the cockpit, then gestured for her to join him. Skin-on-skin contact soon made her worry less about the cold and more about spontaneous combustion.

Erik had said he wouldn't push her into a physical relationship, yet, at the moment, she couldn't remember why it was a bad idea. She wasn't the type of person who jumped into bed with people she'd just met. In fact, she'd known Jean-Claude for almost a year before they'd become intimate. However, she'd known Erik for ten years; it wasn't as if they were strangers.

"Feeling warmer?"

How easy it would be to press a kiss against his chest and then work her way up to his lips. She could feel his arousal against her stomach, so she knew the same lusty thoughts were racing through Erik. His hot breath in her ear melted the last of her willpower. Damn the future, and the past for that matter, for once she was going to seize the day.

As she ran her lips over his collarbone, she heard a loud voice call Erik's name and footsteps on the dock approach the boat. She scurried out of Erik's arms and huddled on the seat across from him. Raising her legs to her chest she wrapped her arms around them.

Erik swore under his breath and sat upright, putting the discarded towel across his lap. "In here, Brent," he called out.

Brent's face appeared in the small gap between the bottom portion of the door and the roof. "I thought I'd come down to check on you. Saw the lake forming in your car and then the boat moored up. When I spoke with Tracy a few minutes ago, she reminded me that she'd taken all the towels and blankets out of the boat for washing. Sorry, I told you it was fully loaded and you didn't need anything."

"We were waiting for the rain to die down a bit before we made a run for the car. If you're here now, maybe you could give us a ride somewhere warm."

"No problem. I'm done for the day. I'll give Tracy a call and let her know I'll be bringing a couple of soaked sailors home with me. Should I ask where your clothes are or keep my mouth shut?"

"I suggest keeping your mouth shut," Erik replied.

He picked up his T-shirt and wrung out the water before handing it to Analise again. The wet fabric clung to her skin, chilling her after the warmth of Erik's embrace. Being held by him was becoming addictive. If she wanted to learn to stand on her own, she'd better find an antidote, and quickly.

Chapter Nine

"So, *Afi*. What do you want to do first?" Analise looked around Gimli's packed harbor area. Three days ago, it had been a scene of quiet tranquility—boats bobbing in the water, a few fishermen on the dock, purple martins darting overhead eating masses of mosquitoes. Today, hordes of people were milling about, looking at display tables, lining up for a taste of local dishes, or waiting for the next installment of entertainment to come on stage.

"I come to *Islendingadagurinn* every year, sweet. You lead the way," he said.

Icelandic Festival days were the biggest thing to happen to the small town each year, a long weekend when the local population celebrated their heritage or just partied it up as small towns did when the carnival arrived.

"Let's grab some *pönnukökur* first, then look at the crafts." Analise walked over to a table where the little rolled-up pancakes filled with sugar were displayed.

The lady behind the table greeted them as they approached. "Hello, Gunnar, how are you? This must be your granddaughter." She was dressed in the traditional Icelandic costume of a long, black dress with a white apron and white hat edged in lace.

"Morning, Inge. Yes, this is Analise. We'll take a

half dozen of the *pönnukökur*, please."

"With pleasure. Can we hope you're back home for good now, Analise?" Inge wrapped the treats in napkins before putting them in a white paper bag.

"I'm not sure," Analise replied.

"Well, it would be lovely if you stayed with your *afi*. We could use more young people around here."

Analise looked around curiously at the young people and families milling about.

"Most of these are from the city or are just here for the summer," Inge continued. "I hear you're engaged to Erik Sigurdson. I know his family would love for him to move back as well."

Ah, the joys of small towns.

"We're talking about it, but we can't make any promises. We both have careers far from here." Her stomach clenched. But she wasn't sure if it was because of the lie or the disappointment the town would feel when she and Erik broke off their fake engagement. If she'd given Jean-Claude back his ring, no one in the world would have cared.

"I heard you were a great photographer. Your *amma* used to show me some of your work. Are you taking photos today for the festival committee?" Inge's voice brought Analise back to the present.

Out of habit, she reached for her camera, which dangled at her side. "No, only for personal use. Thanks for the *pönnukökur*, Inge. May I take your photo before I go?"

"Of course, anything for Gunnar's family."

Analise snapped a photo of Inge surrounded by the

tasty delights. She'd get her granddad to pass on a copy to the friendly woman. They wandered past several crafts tables. She occasionally stopped to admire a particular piece of artwork or ask a question. Almost everyone knew Gunnar and exchanged greetings with him, encouraging her to move back to Akureyri with Erik. Rather than consider it prying, she took the interest in her future as friendly concern and a sincere desire to have her live in the area again.

From the craft tables they made their way over to the beach area. The waves lapped at the sand in a hushed murmur, so different from the crashing tumult that had ended her day of sailing with Erik during the week. Still, soaking aside, it had been about as close to a perfect day as she could remember.

Her thigh didn't hurt anymore, unless she bumped it. And her spirit was healing, too. She woke each morning, eager for the day. When was the last time that had happened?

Yesterday, Erik had been conscripted into taking his mother and grandmother into Winnipeg for a little shopping. Analise had spent the day trying not to think about how much she missed being with him. The physical attraction was becoming something more, and it frightened her.

"Analise!"

She turned at the sound of her name being called. Brent and his children were playing in the sand, attempting a sandcastle. Further along the beach, professionally created, massive sand structures were being judged. The children's handiwork might not have been as impressive, but just as much determination was going into its production. Analise snapped a few pictures after getting Brent's permission. She loved the grainy texture of the sand on the children's small, soft hands—it would make a great black-and-white photograph.

"Where's Erik?" Brent looked around, as if expecting to see him appear any minute.

"He's helping his mother and grandparents set up for the big party tomorrow. He'll meet me here later," she replied. It was disconcerting how everyone expected the two of them to be joined at the hip, probably literally more than figuratively.

"Daddy, we need more water; the sand won't stick." Brent's little boy, Nathan, tugged on his father's arm.

"We'll let you get on with your masterpiece," she said. "I hope you win the competition," she called out as the small child poured the water over the pile of sand his sister had erected, destroying the structure. A wail went up that could probably be heard in Akureyri. Analise left Brent to sort out his domestic dispute.

After wandering around the sand sculptures, they returned to the stage area where students were reciting Icelandic stories. Gunnar sat and closed his eyes, a look of contentment on his face. Even after all these years living in Canada, speaking English, it must have felt like home to hear his native language spoken, even if by amateurs.

Her father, when he was around during her first fifteen years in France, spoke French, and her mother spoke only English. Yet it was hearing Icelandic, the language that her grandparents had used when they didn't think she was listening, that made her feel at peace. She'd never learned it beyond a few basic expressions, but it always soothed her soul. Probably because she associated the language with love.

She took her grandfather's rough hand in hers and closed her eyes as well, letting the reading flow over her like a warm bath. The next thing she knew, her head was pulled gently onto a large shoulder, and a strong arm wrapped around her, supporting her weight. Her eyelids felt as though they were weighted when she tried to open them. Erik's deep voice filled her mind. "Rest, my darling. I'll hold you until you wake."

I am finally home.

***

Analise stirred in his arms, her dark lashes fluttering like a butterfly about to take flight. When her bright aqua eyes gazed up into his, he wasn't prepared for the rush of emotion that swept through him. His chest swelled, and a tumultuous feeling invaded his stomach. Falling in love with Analise was not part of his plan. In fact, given the recent loss of her fiancé, which probably clouded her ability to form any new attachments, it was a disaster. He couldn't afford another ten years getting over her.

"When did you get here?" she mumbled.

"Just as you were about to tumble out of your chair, fast asleep," he answered. "Are you ill? Do you want me to take you home?"

She stretched her arms above her head, pulling her T-shirt taut across her full breasts. He tried to take his eyes off the lace outline of her bra. He tried not to remember the taste of her skin, the low moan that had escaped her lips as he'd drawn her nipple into his mouth. He tried and failed—epically.

"No, I'm fine," she replied, bringing his eyes back up to her lips. Soft, luscious lips. No longer chapped, they practically begged for his kisses.

Man, he needed to get a grip, and fast, before he embarrassed himself in front of all these people.

"Where's *Afi*?" Analise looked around for her grandfather.

"He met up with a friend, and they've gone for a coffee. I told him I'd look after you and take you home."

"I can't go home yet. I haven't been on any rides." She pouted and somehow managed to look even sexier, and another tsunami of lust rolled over him.

"All right, we'll wander over to the park. But you have to promise not to fall asleep on the Sizzler."

"I promise. I'm good to go now. How long was I asleep anyway?"

"About forty minutes in my arms."

"I hope I didn't put off any of the performers."

The performers hadn't had to cope with her soft breath blowing down a gap in his shirt. "I don't think they noticed," he replied. They'd better get walking while he still could.

They wandered down the path by the beach.

Neighbors and friends of his grandparents chatted with them. He kept his arm around Analise, except for when she stopped to take a photo. After replacing her lens cap, she'd return to his side as if it were the most natural place for her to be. And it was.

"I want a huge plate of perogies," she said as they approached the food tent. "With sour cream and bacon and onions."

"Is there any other way to eat perogies?" They lined up behind an elderly woman who turned at the sound of his voice.

"That you, Erik Sigurdson?"

"Yes, ma'am." He scanned the wrinkled face before him, wracking his brain for a connection, but came up blank.

"I remember you when you were just a little thing. This your girlfriend?"

"My fiancée," he corrected. "This is Analise Thordarson."

"Oh, yes, Gunnar Thordarson's granddaughter. I must say we were all so happy, Analise, when you first came to live with your grandparents. They were devastated when Sigrid went to France, taking you with her. Such a surprise, too, as everyone expected Sigrid was going to marry Derek Sigurdson."

"My father?" Erik had never heard that his dad and Analise's mother had been an item.

"Oh, yeah. They were all over each other through high school. Then, when that Frenchie came to town, Sigrid dropped your father like a hot potato and went off with him. I guess it all comes around in the end, if both their children are now getting hitched."

Having made that pronouncement, the lady turned back and ordered her meal, ignoring the shocked look he was sure must be all over his face.

"Did you know about that?" he whispered into Analise's ear.

"Nope, news to me. Now I know why my granddad keeps asking me if I've changed my mind."

"And have you?" The words were out before he could stop them. He was having trouble remembering that their engagement was simply for appearance's sake.

"Not for the week or so, anyway," she said, then stood on tiptoe and gave him a kiss on the cheek.

"What can I get you, dear?" the lady behind the table asked, holding a Styrofoam plate in her hand. Analise ordered and then waited for him to get his dinner.

Laden with perogies, they found a couple of empty spots at a picnic table. Their fellow diners were deep in conversation about what to do with the rest of their time before heading back to Winnipeg.

"Did you know that lady in the food line?" Analise licked a spot of sour cream off the corner of her lips.

Erik took a long drink of his ice-cold lemonade before replying. "No. But I quickly learned that in a small area, who you know and who knows you are usually two wildly different demographics."

"Doesn't it bother you—complete strangers knowing your business?"

"It used to, when I was young. Now I realize most

people are pretty friendly and just want the best for me and my family. Plus, they only know the things I want them to know. Secrets are still possible." He twirled the ring on her finger.

Half an hour later, Analise rubbed her stomach. "I'm stuffed. I always feel such a traitor having Ukrainian food at the Icelandic festival, but I have to say, aside from *pönnukökur* and *vinnaterta,* there's not a lot of Icelandic fare I enjoy. Plus, perogies are pure comfort food."

"Do you feel in need of comfort?" He'd been amazed that she'd gone back for three plates of dinner.

"No, not really. I have been craving potatoes and pasta lately. I guess I lived on rice and couscous for too long."

"Well, you'll get your fill of perogies, potato salad, and pasta tomorrow. The food has already started arriving for the family reunion. I think we could probably feed the entire Interlake region."

"I think the entire Interlake has been invited. I thought the family party was last weekend. So if this thing tomorrow is only your relatives, what's the party next weekend?"

"Last weekend was the super-close family—people my grandparents see on a regular basis. Tomorrow is everyone. My grandmother is one of fourteen, my grandfather comes from a family of five. All their siblings were prolific breeders as well, so I have literally hundreds of cousins, and of course most of them are on the third or fourth generation. There will probably be a couple hundred people there tomorrow."

"And next week?"

"Next week is for the friends and close family. That event is being held at the hotel and is catered. There will probably be about two hundred to that one as well."

"Goodness. You Sigurdsons don't do anything in half measure, do you?"

If only she knew how thoroughly he wanted to make love to her. "Nope. Now, do you want me to win you a giant teddy bear?"

"Of course."

***

Analise hugged the giant bear tightly. Erik had been determined to win the biggest one there, not resting until he'd achieved it. Which probably wouldn't have taken so long if he hadn't had to stop playing every five minutes to introduce her to a vast multitude. Half the festival's attendees seemed to be related to him. She hoped these people didn't expect her to remember their names when she saw them again tomorrow.

The sweet smell of cotton candy and caramel apples filled the air. Children's laughter and the excited screams of those on the rides competed with the call of the carnival workers to come try their games. It was a cacophony of happiness.

"Has your meal digested enough to go on the rides now?" Erik smiled down at her.

"Actually, I'm feeling a bit queasy again. How about we do the Ferris wheel? That should be gentle enough."

Erik tilted his head back and looked at the large ride.

"Um, I'm not too good with heights. If you want to go, I'll hold your bear and wait for you here," he offered.

"You're scared of heights?" She couldn't believe self-assured Erik had a phobia.

"What can I say? I'm a prairie boy. Any elevation over three meters makes me nervous."

"Well, Ferris wheels are no fun on your own. I'm tired, and tomorrow will be a big day. Okay if you take me home now?"

"Absolutely. I've been waiting all day for a few minutes alone with you."

Her heart rate sped up even while her brain tried to convince her body it was a bad idea. Like it had a chance.

"Analise?"

She turned at the sound of a man calling her name. Erik stiffened beside her as a blond-haired man carrying a sleeping child sauntered over to her. Analise wracked her brain until she came up with a name. Then she tensed, as well. Erik's arm tightened around her.

Last time she'd seen Ian MacEwan, he'd been laughing at her best friend, Karen, in the high-school cafeteria. The handsomest guy in school, a jock with his own posse. He'd asked her out a dozen times, but she'd been too infatuated with Erik to even consider it.

The past ten years, however, hadn't been kind to him. Now, he was a little overweight, and his hair was thinning so that she could see a distinct patch of scalp. His green eyes were clouded with failure. A defeated man. It seemed karma hadn't let him get away with his mistreatment of Karen.

"Hello, Ian," she said. If Erik got any more rigid, he'd snap. Did he think she was attracted to the guy? Not in this lifetime.

"I'm surprised to see you here. I didn't know you'd moved back," Ian said. His gaze swept over her, and then he quickly looked away. "This is my wife, Melissa." Ian drew forward a pretty, brown-haired woman.

The two women shook hands before Melissa returned hers to the stroller, where a sleeping toddler was blissfully unaware of the tension between the adults. Another child, a girl about six years old, held on to the side of the pushchair and looked longingly at the bear in Analise's arm.

"I'm only here on holiday," Analise said. Erik seemed struck mute, though he was scowling. What was wrong with him?

"Analise and I are engaged," he said at last.

"Congratulations." Ian rubbed his hand down his pant leg, then held it out, but Erik didn't take it.

Awkward. Analise shook it instead, just to get the moment over with.

Ian cleared his throat. "Well, it was nice to see you again. We have to get the kids to bed. Enjoy your holiday."

Analise forced a smile onto her face. "Good to see you, too, Ian. And it was nice to meet you, Melissa.

You have a beautiful family."

"Thanks," Melissa answered. They moved away, although the little girl continued to stare wistfully at the giant bear.

"Wait," Analise called. She hurried over to the family, leaving Erik standing like a telephone poll in the middle of the fairground. She bent down in front of the child. "I can't take this on the plane back to France with me. Would you look after him? Keep him safe and warm and give him lots of cuddles?"

The little girl put her arms out to take the bear Analise offered but then looked up at her mother. "Can I? Please, Mom."

"I guess it would be all right. Thank you," Melissa said. Ian looked uncomfortable but didn't object.

Analise was rewarded with a radiant smile from the child.

"I'll look after him. Thank you so much. This is the best day ever," the girl said. Her eyes shone like she'd just been handed a tiara full of real diamonds.

"You're welcome," Analise replied. "Good night."

A tear escaped and fell on her empty arm. What the hell was she crying about now? She seriously needed to get some rest. Erik joined her as the family left the park, and she leaned into his strong body. "I hope you don't mind that I gave the bear away."

"No, that's fine. I didn't know Ian had so many children." He avoided her gaze.

She should have asked him first before she gave away his present. But it was the symbolism of him winning something for her that she wanted, not the actual bear. It definitely wouldn't fit into her camera case when she got back to her real life. Although, what life did she really have to go back to? She'd seen more than her share of death and destruction. She wouldn't go back to photojournalism.

"You okay?" She put her hand on Erik's cheek as he continued to stare off into the distance. Finally, his blue gaze met hers, a hint of regret in his eyes.

"Yes, sorry. All these faces from the past are hard to keep up with."

"Ian's three years younger than you. I didn't realize you knew him before."

"I only knew him in passing. I think we played on the same baseball team at some point. Come on, let's get you home. You look really tired."

Looks don't lie. Who knew juggling all these past and present emotions was so exhausting?

Erik was unusually quiet on the drive home and seemed lost in his own thoughts. She put a hand on his arm as they approached her grandfather's place. "Did my grandfather say anything to you on Wednesday when you picked me up to go sailing?"

"About what?"

"About his property?"

He glanced over at her before returning his gaze to the road. "He offered to change the title deed over to our names."

"I thought as much. He's mentioned that to me as well. I keep telling him no, that it's his place. With my grandmother gone, though, I don't think he wants to stay there."

"Where would he go?"

"I think he's just waiting to die. He's made me promise that when he goes I have him cremated and then the ashes put in with my grandma." She couldn't help the tear that trickled down her face.

Erik parked in front of the house and turned the engine off, although he made no effort to get out of the vehicle. He turned his full attention on her, reaching out and wiping another stray tear with the pad of his thumb.

"His grief is still raw. Give him some time. I'm sure he'll learn to adjust, especially with you here."

"I don't know, Erik. He and my grandmother were so close. I can only image what it must be like to lose someone you've spent almost your whole life with. But he's all I have left."

"He knows that, Analise. And he loves you. He won't do anything…" She appreciated him not ending the sentence. With both her mother and his sister taking their own lives, it was difficult to find the right word for such an act of desperation.

"It's like he's given up on life. I've heard of people dying of heartbreak before. I'm worried that if he thinks we are really together, he'll fade away, feeling that now I have you, he can let go. Can't I tell him that our engagement is just a ruse to keep your family off your back?"

"No," Erik blurted out before continuing more gently, "I think that would hurt him too much, having deceived him in the first place. We'll have to make sure we tell him how much we want him a part of our lives."

"I guess the engagement will be over soon, anyway. Then he'll want to live on to help me over the pain." She didn't need to tell Erik the inevitability of pain was becoming stronger each day. She was a little surprised, however, when he made no comment on the timing of their breakup.

Instead, he undid his seatbelt and leaned over to her. He kissed her so sweetly, another tear escaped. Pulling back a fraction he searched her eyes. "I am going to make you a promise, right here, right now. No matter what happens or doesn't happen between us, you'll never be alone. You will always be a part of me, part of my family."

He kissed her again, and she almost believed him.

Chapter Ten

Another wave of nausea swelled within Analise. Having thrown up everything she'd eaten, her stomach was empty. But that didn't stop the heaves. She pressed her forehead against the cool bathroom wall. Fortunately, her grandfather had taken his second cup of morning coffee out onto the porch, and it was unlikely he'd have heard her retching from the front of the house.

She tried to convince herself that it was eating too many perogies at the fair yesterday … or that the milk tasted funny in her cereal this morning. She was too much of a realist, though, to believe any of those scenarios for long. If she'd had a fever, she could try to persuade herself that it was malaria or some other tropical disease she'd picked up in her travels. But she had none of those symptoms. And the excuse that she hadn't had a period because of the recent stress and trauma in her life wasn't cutting it, either.

As she sipped a glass of cold water in the kitchen, she glanced at the clock on the stove. She had almost two hours before she had to be at Erik's grandparents' farm. Brent and Tracy were going to pick her up on their way to save another car to park.

If she hurried, she still had enough time to go to the pharmacy before she had to get ready. She daren't go to one in Akureyri; too many people recognized her now, and Gimli was too busy with the festival. She'd have to drive over to Arborg.

Fighting the desire to hurl again, she grabbed her bag and keys and headed out the door. Time to get a stick and pee on it.

Mission accomplished, she sat on the edge of her mattress and watched the little indicator window proudly proclaim her pregnant. Analise lay back on the bed and stared at the ceiling. This was not something she'd ever imagined happening. She'd faithfully taken the pill every day until he'd died, knowing Jean-Claude would never want a child—never want the responsibility, never want to be tied down. She glanced at the stick again. Her late fiancé had given her one more surprise. Even in death, he still managed to control her life.

Her hand flitted over her still-flat belly. Flat for now. A little life grew inside, a new start. Her child. A wave of warmth and possessiveness overrode the nerves and trepidation. She was going to be a mom. And she was going to be the best damn mom, ever.

Her phone pinged with an incoming text.

Erik: Can't wait till you get here. I've hidden a whole bowl of perogies just for you.

The mom thing would have to wait. For now, she had to play the part of fake fiancée.

Analise sat up, grabbed her dress, and headed for the shower. She had forty-five minutes to get ready for the Sigurdson party. Her pregnancy was a complication she hadn't reckoned on in her pretend engagement. Hopefully, she'd be able to keep it secret until she left Manitoba.

Right on time, Brent and Tracy arrived to pick her up. Analise had carefully done her makeup, trying to hide the ravages of her earlier nausea. She put on a fake smile, to match her fake ring given to her by her fake fiancé, and greeted the family like she hadn't seen them in years. Too soon, they were at the farm, surrounded by hundreds of people.

Analise shifted her weight from one foot to the other. How could one person possibly have so much family? Her cheeks hurt from constantly smiling for the past two hours, accepting congratulations on her engagement and welcomes to the family. Erik's arm seemed permanently fused to her waist. As if sensing her malaise, he kept asking if she was okay.

"I'm starting to worry about you, my love. Do you think it's time you saw a doctor?"

A doctor's appointment would be the perfect excuse to go into Winnipeg to meet the Yemeni contact. "You could be right. I'll try to book something for later in the week."

Erik put a hand to her face and stared into her eyes. His blue gaze seemed to look right into her heart. Before he could discover her secret, she looked away. Fortunately, one of Erik's endless cousins stood beside them, waiting to speak.

"Analise, I know it's your job, and you're here on holiday ... but I notice you have your camera. Would you mind taking a picture of my family?" Erik's cousin, Leslie, asked.

"Sure, no problem." She pulled out of Erik's arms and swung her camera up to her eye before he could respond.

After that, it was a series of photo opportunities. She'd planned on giving Erik's grandparents an album of family photos for an anniversary gift, and this gave her the chance to take some candid as well as posed shots. She switched to taking photos unobserved with a long lens—capturing genuine emotion and not the practiced smiles of staged photos. It was her forte.

Her stomach rumbled, but she ignored it. She was in the zone and had often gone twelve hours without eating when working.

"There you are." Erik's voice made her jump.

Swiveling around, she spied her fake fiancé leaning against the porch railing. In each hand, he had a paper plate heaped with food. Analise put the lens cap on, replaced the camera in her bag, and approached. He got full marks for playing the attentive lover.

As soon as she stepped within two feet of him, the smell of the food caused another wave of nausea.

"Excuse me. I need to go to the bathroom first," she managed to get out.

Pushing past him, she ran into the house. Thankfully, the bathroom was empty, as most of the guests were still lining up at the buffet tables.

She made it just in time, without a second to spare to lock the door.

After she had emptied her stomach for the second

time that day, she sat on the floor, pressing her sweating brow to the cool edge of the bathtub.

She was about to leverage herself off the floor when the door flew open. A woman wearing a flower-print dress, thick-soled black shoes, and her hair pulled back into a severe bun stood in the doorway. She took one look at Analise, another at the raised toilet seat, and had a light-bulb moment.

"You're pregnant!" She almost did a dance as she pronounced the diagnosis.

Damn, I could have saved ten bucks on the test.

As the woman turned and ran from the room, Analise belatedly recognized her as one of Erik's second cousins. The one he'd whispered was the biggest gossip in the family.

"Nooo!" Analise called out too late. "It's stomach flu!"

Time must have slowed somehow, because by the time she'd scrambled to her feet and made it out of the room, there was no sign of the woman. Analise swished her mouth out with a handful of water, then pinched her cheeks, hoping to give her face a little color.

When she stepped out onto the back porch, it seemed every eye turned in her direction. The general buzz of conversation stilled. If this scene were playing out in an Old West movie, a tumbleweed would have rolled by or ominous organ music played. She scanned the sea of faces staring at her and caught a glimpse of the woman she'd seen briefly from the floor. The cousin had a huge grin like she'd scored the biggest scoop of the century. Erik's mother stood next to him, her face flushed and her jaw clenched. Erik himself blinked once, then plastered on a tight smile. Putting the paper plate he still held for her down on a nearby table, his eyes never left her face. Everyone at the gathering watched as he approached her.

"Love, come sit down in the house where it's quiet. I'll get you a glass of water." Erik's voice was loud enough for all to hear, his grip on her elbow firm yet gentle. "I told you to lie down if you weren't feeling well," he added in a stage whisper as they entered the house.

Dazed, Analise followed him into his grandparents' small sitting room. Crocheted protectors sat on the arms and backs of the chairs; the sofa was adorned with a handmade, knit afghan in a plethora of colors. It was a room where myriad family discussions had taken place. But she was fairly certain no sham engagements had been dissolved on the discovery that the fake fiancée was carrying another man's child. Erik led her over to the sofa and gestured for her to sit.

"You're pregnant?" The question was gently phrased, but his eyes bore into hers.

"Yes," she whispered.

To his credit, he handled the shock well. "I would have appreciated a little heads-up. My cousin congratulated my mother, who immediately demanded to know why I hadn't told her first. I could hardly say it was because it was news to me."

He paced the tiny room, looming over her.

"I'm sorry. I just did the test this morning. We haven't had a moment alone since I got here." She really should have made the time to tell him. *Nice party. By the way, I'm pregnant with my dead fiancé's baby.* Her only excuse was that she was still trying to get her head around the discovery herself.

"You realize that everyone assumes the baby is mine."

She swallowed. "I know. But if you tell them it isn't, we'll have the perfect excuse to end this pretense."

"No." His voice was firm. He stood in front of her, hands on his hips, his lips pulled into a firm line.

"What do you mean, 'no'?"

"We aren't getting un-engaged. We're getting married."

***

The tiny bit of color in her face disappeared at his words. Her gaze narrowed as if she couldn't believe what he'd just said. He could hardly believe it himself. But having said the words, he couldn't take them back—didn't want to take them back.

"Erik, you can't be serious. We hardly know each other. This engagement was to be a temporary thing, to appease your family during your grandparents' celebrations. By the end of next week we are to part company for good."

The room was too small for any decent pacing, so he sat next to Analise. Her hand shook in her lap, and he took it in his. "Listen, Analise. I don't think you realize how complicated this situation is for you now, here."

"I'm a single mom. I think even in Akureyri they can grasp that concept."

"To every person out there," he nodded toward the back of the house, "and by now probably half the population of Manitoba, you are carrying *my* baby. If I deny it, it will blacken your name forever. Every time you or your child came here, they would talk about how you had an affair with another man while engaged to me."

"What if I don't want to come back here?"

Erik searched her eyes. "I don't think that's true. I think the longer you're here, the more you understand this is the place you're meant to be. What's waiting for you back in Paris, Analise? A tiny apartment, a congested city? What kind of place is that to raise a child? Here, you have fresh air and space. And your baby will be loved by an entire community."

"But only if I marry you."

"Marrying me will certainly help. You might not have noticed, I'm quite popular." He tried to smile, but she looked too worried to respond to his tease.

"But you don't have plans to stay. Do you suggest we marry and then you go off to London or Toronto and I stay here?" Her aqua eyes swam in unshed tears. Was she upset about the baby or the prospect of him leaving? His heart pounded, and his mouth went dry.

"I've been thinking about returning here myself." Since wandering around the fair with her yesterday, he'd been contemplating how enjoyable a quiet life in the country could be, with Analise. It may not provide the same challenge of working in a world-class city, but even rural people needed good legal counsel. She didn't look convinced, however, so he continued. "While I've enjoyed my time in Europe, working eighteen-hour days six or seven days a week isn't really living. Being back here has reminded me that a simpler life has its merits, as well. I've proved I can make it with the big boys. Now I want to prove I can be a good man—a good husband … and father."

"You can't mean this, Erik. I appreciate what you're saying; however, I need to decide what's best for my baby. I'm not sure a marriage of convenience is it."

The slamming of the back screen door warned them they were no longer alone. He stood, ready to shield Analise from whomever had entered. She seemed to be one person away from a complete breakdown.

"Knock, knock," his mother's slurred voice rang out.

He drew in a deep breath before answering. "We're in here, Mom." Although, he needn't have bothered, as she was already standing in the doorway.

"Are you okay, dears? Your announcement was quite the surprise. I wish you would have told me first rather than let me hear it from Corinna Perkins." The censure in her voice was negated as she held on to the doorframe for support.

"Sorry, we were hoping to keep it quiet until after Gran and Gramps' anniversary party next week. We didn't want to overshadow their celebration." Good, the news sounded like it was old to him, rather than the ten minutes he'd had to adjust to the monumental shift in his relationship, real or pretend, with Analise.

"Are you kidding? They're over the moon. They're so excited that another little Sigurdson is going to join the family."

Erik caught sight of Analise swallowing. She seemed about to say something, possibly to correct his mother as to the child's last name.

"There are hundreds of Sigurdsons outside already," he interjected before Analise could say anything.

"Yes, but you've always been a favorite grandson. I know they're hoping you'll come back here permanently and take over the farm. Now that you have a baby on the way, it would be a perfect time to come home for good."

"Mom, this is something Analise and I have to decide for ourselves. I'm going to take her back to Gunnar's house so she can rest. Please tell Gran and Gramps I'm sorry to leave. I'll be back in an hour or so."

"Really? Do you have to go? There's so much to sort out. Of course, you'll have to get married before the baby comes. When are you due, Analise? Oh, wouldn't it be amazing if it's on Karen's birthday?"

One glance at Analise told him she'd had enough. Her hand was over her mouth, her eyes darting to the door and back. If this whole thing wasn't going to explode in his face, he had to get her away from his mother.

"Mom, remember what I said about giving us some space. If I'm not back in time to set up the music for dancing, ask Brent to do it. He's handy with a computer."

"Oh, all right." His mother left, and he heard a long sigh behind him.

He turned to Analise, who looked like she'd rather melt into the sofa. As she stood, he wrapped his arms around her. She snuggled against his chest, and he tightened his arms. If there weren't 200 people outside, he would have held her like this for the rest of the night. But if he didn't appear soon, they'd all troop in, and that was the last thing Analise needed. "Did you only bring your camera bag or do you have a handbag somewhere as well?"

"Just my camera bag. Do you think I should say good-bye to your grandparents? I don't want to be rude."

Erik put a hand on Analise's face before bestowing a gentle kiss on her lips.

"They won't think you're rude. If we go out back again, you'll be inundated by people asking you questions about the baby and when it's due. Do you really want to face that?"

A shudder coursed through her. "No. As long as your grandparents don't mind, I think I need to lie down at home in the quiet."

He steered Analise out the front, intending to make her comfortable in his car while he retrieved her camera. Unfortunately, whoever had organized the parking hadn't thought about anyone other than the last to arrive wanting to leave. As he tried to figure out how he was going to get his car out from behind the twenty-five others parked in front of it, Brent appeared from around the corner of the house.

"Tracy figured you'd want to leave. Here's Analise's bag." His cousin surveyed the haphazard parking arrangement and pulled his keys from his pocket. "Take my car," he offered, tossing them to Erik. "I must say, your little surprise announcement has set the whole party abuzz. Uncle Arni is already taking bets on gender and due date. Got any insider information I can use to improve my odds?"

"Not yet. Thanks for the loan of the car—I'll be back soon."

"No hurry. We'll be here for hours yet. I hope you feel better soon, Analise. When Tracy was expecting our first, she threw up on the hour every hour for the first five months."

"*Mon Dieu*," Analise groaned. She looked like she might be sick again any moment.

He took the heavy bag from Brent and placed it on his own shoulder. He was surprised Analise could carry it around as though it were a piece of paper. She was definitely stronger than she looked. He'd have to remember that. Looking down at her now, however, pale and a little disoriented, he knew she needed his strength. "Let's get you to bed."

"Ha, ha! That's what got you in this mess in the first place," Brent replied with a laugh. He was still chuckling when he disappeared around the corner.

"I can't believe this is happening," Analise said as

he pulled Brent's car onto the road. "What is my grandfather going to say? We have to tell him the truth."

As soon as they were out of sight of the house, he pulled over. This conversation required his full concentration.

"We do. We'll tell him that you're pregnant."

"I mean the truth about the fake engagement."

He took a deep breath, trying to get his swirling emotions to sit still for a second while he reasoned with her. "Analise, I meant what I said back at the house. I believe we should get married." She opened her mouth to protest, and he put a finger on her lips. "At least consider it. We can talk more tomorrow after you've had time to think. My solution will save your reputation and stop the gossip. And if our engagement becomes real, why bother your grandfather with the timing now?"

God, that had to be the worst proposal ever— marry me and people won't talk about you behind your back.

"I guess you're right." She didn't look convinced.

He resisted the urge to press his case. If she ran away again...

After turning the key in the ignition, he automatically glanced into the rearview mirror. Two empty car seats—littered with chip fragments, an assortment of Cheerios and Fruit Loops, and one incredibly squashed juice box—stared back at him.

He closed his eyes for a second, recording the moment realization hit, then put the car in gear, and drove. When he stopped Brent's car in front of the Thordarson home, Gunnar stepped out of the house and stood on the porch, surprised to see them so soon.

"Everything all right? I didn't expect you back till after midnight."

"Analise isn't feeling well. She needs quiet and rest," Erik replied as he opened the passenger door and helped her out.

Gunnar looked his granddaughter up and down. "I thought she didn't look too good when she left. I hope it's not some disease you caught taking pictures of those starving babies in Africa."

"No, although a baby is to blame," Erik clarified as he put his arm around her waist. "Analise is expecting."

Analise stiffened but didn't say anything.

"Congratulations, sweet." Gunnar made an attempt to sound genuinely pleased, but it didn't make it to his blue eyes, which were filled with worry.

"Thanks, *Afi*. It's been a bit of a shock to me. I still haven't quite got my head around it. Do you mind if we don't talk about the baby just now?"

"Not at all. Come inside. I'll make you some peppermint and ginger tea. Your *amma* swore it was the only thing that helped with nausea."

Analise removed Erik's hand from her waist and, after giving him a chaste kiss on the cheek, said, "Go back to the party. I'll be fine. See you tomorrow."

She joined her grandfather on the porch and waved to Erik as he climbed back into the car. He drove halfway back to the farm, then stopped again on the deserted gravel road. Shutting off the engine, he let the stillness envelope him. In five minutes, he'd be back at the party, slapped on the back and congratulated or called a dog for getting his fiancée pregnant before the wedding. He'd have to look chagrined, feign remorse, and take it all with a smile on his face.

In reality, he wanted to get stinking drunk and punch something. He didn't know which was worse: knowing the baby wasn't his, or the complication that the pregnancy would bring to his future.

But it was his responsibility. If he didn't fix this, he'd never be able to face any of his family again—wouldn't be able to look himself in the mirror. He'd caused this mess by convincing Analise to pretend to be his fiancée. Now he had to make it right.

Chapter Eleven

"How are you feeling this morning, sweet?"

Analise sat in her grandmother's rocking chair and cradled a mug of peppermint and ginger tea. A soft breeze swayed the crop of grain in the neighbor's field. Three birds rode a thermal updraft, soaring without effort. They were too far away to tell what kind they were, but she admired their worry-free existence.

"Much better, thanks, *Afi*. A good night's sleep has worked wonders. I've even managed to keep my breakfast in today. Well, at least so far," she added with a grimace, as a flicker of nausea reared its ugly head. She took a quick sip of her tea, hoping to hold off the need to hurl.

"Erik called while you were in the shower. Said he'd be over about ten."

"Oh, okay." She took a long drink of her tea, hiding her face from her observant grandfather. Erik had been all concern and solicitude yesterday, but now that he'd had the night to think about their situation, she wasn't sure if he'd continue to insist that they marry. Maybe he was going to tell her that their pretense was over. A wave of despair washed through her. As much as she'd tried to pretend she didn't care for him, it wasn't true. But could she marry him knowing he was just offering as a way to get them out of the sticky mess he'd created? What if she fell for him even more and when the time came to split she was left as broken as her mother had been?

"Analise?"

She turned to face her grandfather. He almost never called her by her given name, unless she was in trouble—which, technically, she was.

"Yes, *Afi*?"

"You don't *have* to marry Erik. There will be no shame, and I won't think any less of you if you decide to raise this child on your own. I'll support you in any way possible, and you know you'll always have a home here."

She put her hand over her grandfather's, which rested on the arm of his rocking chair. "Thank you." This is what she needed: love without an agenda.

"I don't want you to end up like your mother," he said, his voice raw with emotion.

The usual guilt sliced through her. For years, she'd carried the burden of feeling responsible for her mother's death; she'd even stopped celebrating her birthday. She and her mother had argued the morning she turned fifteen. Analise had wanted to take the train into Paris with her friends and do some shopping. Her mother had wanted her to come home and spend the afternoon and evening with her. Her father, as usual, was somewhere else and hadn't even called to wish her a happy day.

After school, she'd delayed, going over to a friend's house for a few hours before returning home. When she'd eventually opened the door to their home, a luxury, stone-walled house in Versailles, it had seemed eerily quiet. A wonky cake sat on the dining-room table, baked and decorated by her mother. Analise had recognized the lopsided writing—how much had her mother had to drink beforehand?

The cook, who was normally bustling about the kitchen, was nowhere to be found. Analise had wandered around the lower floor—usually there was music playing or the television was on as Sigrid hated absolute quiet, said it gave her too much time to think. When even the garden was empty, Analise had eventually gone up to her mother's room, thinking perhaps she was taking a nap or had passed out.

Sure enough, Sigrid was lying on her bed, eyes closed. As Analise was about to shut the bedroom door and go back downstairs to get herself some dinner, something caught her eye. She was never sure what it was—a flash of sunlight on the overturned bottle of vodka on the floor or the awkward angle of her mother's legs? Whatever it was, it had made her turn back. And when she'd walked fully into the room, her eyes had become fixed on the empty bottle of pills on the bedside table, a single tablet in her mother's open palm.

The scream lodged in her throat never made it out. Grasping her mother's hand, she'd found it was already cold. If only she'd come home on time. If only she hadn't fought with her mother. If only she'd realized how sad and lonely her mother was.

If only had haunted Analise for years.

The creak of her grandfather's chair brought her

back to the present. Her hand rested on her stomach as if protecting the little life that grew there. "I won't, *Afi*. I know my strengths and weaknesses. And I promise if I ever feel the desperation my mother must have felt to do what she did, I'll seek help. I know what it's like to be the one left behind. I wouldn't do that to my baby or you."

"I just wanted you to know you have options, sweet," he said after clearing his throat. "There's something not right about your relationship with Erik. I don't know what it is, and I guess it's not my place to pry…"

"You're not prying. I know you want the best for me. Erik and I … well, we have a lot of issues to resolve. We jumped into this engagement without thinking it through. I love him, but I'm not sure I can live the life he wants. And I guess now my pregnancy complicates rather than clarifies the situation. But I'm a big girl, *Afi*. I've looked after myself for ten years. And if it comes to it, I'll look after my child by myself as well."

"That's my girl. But I don't think you'll have to. Here comes your man now."

After bumping along the drive, the BMW convertible pulled up in front of the house. The top was up, so she had to wait until Erik stepped out of the vehicle to see his face. His somber expression turned into a smile. Analise wasn't sure, though, if the smile was for her or her grandfather's benefit.

"Well, I reckon you two have a lot to talk about, and you don't need an old man around. I'm going to go down to the stables and check on things. I hear Ian MacEwan might have to get rid of some of his horses. Think I might take on a few more and get back into the riding-lesson business." *Afi* pushed himself to his feet and, after nodding at Erik, strode toward the barns, whistling. Analise stared after her grandfather, pleased to see a spark of life back in him.

Erik leaned against the porch rail and scrutinized her.

"You look better today," he pronounced. His gaze lingered for a moment on her lips before lowering to her stomach. When his eyes returned to hers there was a warmth in them that surprised her. Could he really be happy about the baby?

"I didn't know I looked so terrible yesterday."

"Not terrible, just ill. How are you feeling?"

"Better, thanks. How did the party go?" It was the stilted conversation of two people avoiding what they really needed to discuss.

"It wasn't the same without you."

"So, I guess we should talk about the baby." She didn't know what to say. It had all seemed so clear in the night. Leave Akureyri, have her baby in France, get on with her life as best she could. Erik had gotten her into this engagement mess, he could get her out. Yet, somehow, with his tall form standing in front of her, the heat of his gaze on her, she was having trouble remembering why she should follow this course.

"The general consensus at the party yesterday was that we should get married right away. In fact, my grandmother suggested we have the wedding next weekend at their anniversary party. Everyone is already invited, the venue is booked and catered. All we'd have to do is get you a dress. One of my aunts has already started on a cake." At least he had the sense to stare at his shoes at the last statement. If he'd been looking at her, she'd have sliced him with her laser-sharp gaze.

"Hold on one minute. Are you actually saying that yesterday, after you dropped me off, you then organized our whole wedding? Without me? I don't recall even agreeing to your proposal. Then again, I said I'd have a coffee with you and wound up engaged. Who knows what you think is acceptance." She jumped from the rocker and stood with her hands on her hips. Unfortunately, the move brought her within touching distance of Erik, who stopped leaning and instead stood straight, narrowing the gap further.

She could feel his breath at the top of her hair; a hint of his manly aftershave tickled her nostrils. And when he pulled her into his arms, her hand automatically rested against his heart, which was beating rapidly under firm chest muscles.

"This is for the best—for you, for the baby, for everyone. I'm not saying we have to stay married forever, just long enough to lend legitimacy to the arrangement. If you agree, the baby can have my name if you like, and I'll support you both for as long as you want. No prenup— everything I have is yours." Risky talk for a lawyer. He must really want to marry her. The question was why?

"Erik, this is insane. It's not your baby. It's not your responsibility. We've barely been together two weeks. Getting married is crazy." Her refusal would have so much more power if she weren't clinging to him like a piece of melted cheese.

"This is my responsibility. You're wearing my ring, whether you agreed to marry me or not. By coercing you into faking the engagement, I've put you in a compromising position. I don't think you understand the long-term effects of breaking off this relationship now. Is the thought of being married to me, even in name only, so horrible?"

"Is that all it's going to be? A marriage in name only?" Okay, who was trying to kid whom now? They could barely keep their hands off each other with just a fake relationship to hold them together. Add a legal document proclaiming them husband and wife and the clothes would be flying before the minister said, "You may now kiss the bride."

"If that's what it will take to get you to agree," Erik promised.

"I need time to think." Because at the moment, the only word repeating through her mind was *yes, yes, yes*. If only he'd say he loved her. But she'd learned long ago that "if onlys" just led to heartache.

"And I need to kiss you. I need you, Analise. Please marry me." He lifted her face with a finger under her chin. Her breath caught as his blue eyes searched hers. The kiss started gentle, but soon his mouth was ravaging hers, imprinting his taste on her brain. When he released her lips, they were both breathing heavily.

"Convinced yet?" he murmured as he nuzzled her

ear.

"To marry you? Or that this marriage can be purely platonic?"

His soft chuckle ran from her ear straight to her heart, warming it. "Both," he replied.

They had want, they had need. This could work. And if it didn't, well, she could always say at least she tried. No "if onlys" to haunt her. "I can't believe I'm saying yes to this. I think I should have a doctor examine my head while she's checking out the rest of me."

Erik raised her head and kissed her so thoroughly she forgot what they had been discussing. When he eventually pulled back, he whispered into her hair, "Let's go to Winnipeg to get you a wedding dress. We can leave a note for your grandfather."

She hauled in a deep breath.

Mon Dieu, I'm getting married.

***

Analise stood in front of the long mirror and sighed. The dress was beautiful, just like she'd imagined when she was a little girl. It was hard to get excited about a wedding, though, when her life was spiraling out of control. Erik sat on a sofa, talking on the phone and watching as the seamstress pinned the dress so that it fit perfectly.

The mermaid hemline and ruched bodice emphasized what little curves she had, although her breasts were already tender and had swollen a little with her pregnancy. Another few weeks, and she probably wouldn't be able to squeeze into the form-fitting dress.

Erik lifted the phone away from his ear. "My gran and mom want to know if there's anyone else you want to invite to the wedding. Your father?"

"No. The only person I care about being there is my granddad."

"Are you sure, love? I know this is sudden. If it makes you feel more comfortable to have some of your other family or friends attend, I can fly them out, but we'll have to make the arrangements today."

She turned and stared back at the mirror. Was her life so empty that there was only one person she cared to have at her wedding? The numbers on Erik's side had already escalated from two to almost 300. She could invite her lawyer who managed her business affairs, or her agent with whom she had a casual friendship, or Therese who lived across the hall from her Paris apartment. However, then she'd have to answer even more awkward questions as to why she was suddenly getting married when all she'd come for was a holiday with her grandfather. No, best to keep this on the down-low. Then it would be so much easier to go back to her normal life when it was all over. She squeezed her eyes shut. There was no normal life to go back to. This was her new reality.

A lump formed in her throat, which she cleared before answering. "No, just *Afi*."

Erik gave her a puzzled look, then went back to the phone, jotting a few notes on a piece of paper. She could hear him fielding several other questions about the arrangements but let her mind transport her to another place. It was a trick she'd learned covering her first war zone with Jean-Claude: pretend what you see through the lens is happening someplace else. It had allowed her to keep her heart—and her hand—still, in order to capture the most evocative images without becoming emotionally involved. Of course, that only worked until she reviewed the photos later, deciding which ones to send for publication. Then, the whole horror of what she'd witnessed would haunt her until the next day, when it was replaced by an equally traumatic scene.

She'd never expected, though, to view her own wedding as a scene to be diffracted and analyzed later. She opened her mouth to tell Erik she couldn't go through with it. But the words died on her tongue when she saw the effort he was putting into making this work. He was doing this for her and her baby. She hadn't stopped to consider what he might be going through at the moment. Surely, marriage to a woman he barely knew carrying another man's baby hadn't been part of his holiday agenda.

He disconnected the call and turned his attention back to her. "Tracy called her obstetrician, and there's been a cancellation for this afternoon if you want the doctor to check you and the baby. If there's someone else you'd rather see, that's okay, too. She just thought it might ease your mind. She said she was terrified when she first discovered she was pregnant and sick all the time, and hearing the doctor say everything was fine really helped."

"Thanks, that would be great." Analise's hand flew to her stomach at the mention of the baby. She wondered when it would sink in that there was a tiny life inside her.

"There, that's done," the seamstress said as she stood back to examine her handiwork. "I can have the dress ready for pick up on Friday if that suits you."

"It's perfect," Erik declared as he, too, stood and examined the effect of the dress on his bride-to-be.

Analise nodded weakly and then stepped off the dais to return to the dressing room. When exactly had she lost all control of her life?

***

Erik sat in the doctor's waiting room, idly flipping through a copy of *Canadian Parent*. He couldn't bear to read any of the articles; it made his current crazy course seem all too real. He'd wanted to accompany Analise in to see the doctor; however, she'd put her foot down and declared she could manage on her own. He was having a hard time remembering that the baby she carried wasn't his. They hadn't even made love, for God's sake. Although he'd thought about it often enough. As much now as ten years ago.

Was he doing the right thing? He wanted Analise, there was no denying that. But now she came as part of a package deal. Was he ready to be a father? Dirty diapers and sleepless nights hadn't actually been in his travel plans. Luxury holidays in the Seychelles would now be family trips to Disneyland.

A blue-eyed, chubby baby wearing only a diaper smiled toothlessly up at him from the magazine in his lap. With its blond hair and fair skin, this could be his child. What if Analise's baby looked like Jean-Claude? Became a constant reminder that he wasn't the father? Was he ready for that?

Damn it all, he had to be. Whatever happened, he'd deal with it. He wasn't going to let Analise go through this alone. Even if she decided, a year from now, that this wasn't what she wanted, he'd respect that decision. Well, he'd try.

To take his mind off his worries, he checked out the other patients in the room. A heavily pregnant woman sat next to her partner, who was reading a golf magazine. She asked him a question, but he just grunted in her direction. Another couple was holding hands and whispering to each other. The woman had a baby names book in her lap. A third woman with a small bump sat by herself, staring out the window.

If he weren't there for Analise, would she be gazing off into the distance, wondering how she'd ended up in this situation, all alone? He'd caught her often enough with her eyes transfixed on a distant object, as though she'd left her body behind and would be back for it later. Where did she go? Back to Jean-Claude? Was she mourning the loss of her baby's father? Imagining him sitting next to her, holding her hand while the doctor ran the tests? Erik gritted his teeth. Jean-Claude was dead; he was here.

"Thank you, Doctor," Analise's soft, sexy voice

called out a moment before she appeared around the corner. The smile she bestowed on Erik was warm and genuine, as though she was glad to see him there. The constriction in his chest eased, and he stood to take her hand.

"Everything all right?"

"Yes. It's still a little early to hear the baby's heartbeat, but everything else seems in order. The doctor's ordered some blood work, so if you don't mind one more stop before we go home, there's a lab around the corner that can do it."

"No problem at all." He waited until they were on the street before he said, "I'm sorry Jean-Claude isn't here to share this with you."

She stopped walking and stared up at him. "Jean-Claude wouldn't have come with me to the doctor. He'd have left me somewhere he considered safe and gone off on his own. A baby would have been a complication, a change of lifestyle he didn't want. I'm sad that he's gone. But if I had to choose anyone to share this with, it would be you."

His heart crawled into his throat. How could any man not want to support his baby's mother? Erik was honored to share this with Analise. "I grew up on a farm, so I saw lots of animals being born. But I still think it a miracle that there is a little life inside you. You're growing a human being. How amazing is that?"

"Absolutely amazing." Analise smiled up at him and took his hand. A sense of well-being flowed through him. All the success of his career—the accolades and bonuses—were nothing compared to the elation he felt when Analise looked at him like that. He would do everything in his power to keep her smiling and relaxed.

An hour later, they were back on the highway. Analise was asleep, her lips parted slightly. Erik clenched his fist in an effort to take his mind off pulling over and kissing her. He'd told her earlier the marriage would be in name only. However, it was one promise he didn't think he'd be able to keep. Every time he was near her, he wanted to make love to her until she couldn't remember anyone except him.

He wrenched his mind back to the reason he'd come to Manitoba in the first place, aside from his grandparents' anniversary. Ian MacEwan. So far, the finance company had called in all their loans, and Erik was busy preventing him from finding other funding. As soon as Ian missed a mortgage payment on his stables, Erik could turn the screws and let him know what it was like to have all your dreams turn to dust in an instant. Yet, the image of Ian with his young family made Erik's stomach roil. He'd been waiting to crush the man who had driven his sister to suicide for so long, it seemed impossible to turn back now.

Victory felt strangely hollow.

Chapter Twelve

Analise stopped by the farmhouse to drop off some dishes. It seemed Erik's family didn't think she and her grandfather were capable of feeding themselves and had taken to sending food parcels with Erik every time he visited, which was daily. She tried to resent the implication that she couldn't look after herself, but the lasagna had been too good to hold on to a grudge for long. Besides, with her near-constant nausea, she hadn't felt like cooking, and her grandfather's skills seemed limited to egg-related dishes. There were only so many omelets she could eat in a week.

Erik came to the door before she was even out of her vehicle. She'd really hoped he'd be helping his grandfather somewhere on the farm and she could make her trip to Winnipeg without his knowing. Or at least not knowing until she was too far down the road to follow. *Tell no one,* the Yemeni contact had said. She didn't know who she was meeting and didn't want to get Erik involved in something that could be a detriment to his career.

The muffled noise of a radio talk show in the other room gave her some hope at least that his mother and grandmother in the next room couldn't overhear their conversation.

"Erik, there's no need for you to come with me

today. I'm only going to pick up the dress and run a few errands. You're going to have to let me out of your sight sometime, you know." Analise put her hands on her hips.

"But it's a long drive to the city, and you're tired." He caressed her cheek.

She dug her fingernails into her palm to stop herself from melting into him. *A spine would come in handy about now.* "I'm fine. Listen, I need a little time alone. I've been surrounded by your family since this whole wedding fiasco erupted—" She saw him wince at the word "fiasco" and softened her tone. He was trying to keep everyone happy. He must've been emotionally exhausted himself. She put a hand on his cheek and feathered a touch over his lips with her thumb. "I'll be fine driving in and out on my own. Besides, I do have a little personal shopping to do. It's my wedding day; I should get a few things for myself. Maybe even a surprise gift for you."

Erik shifted his weight from one foot to the other, obviously trying to decide whether she was going to try to make a run for it or if she genuinely had some personal matters to attend to. Finally, he relented.

"All right, but for my peace of mind, will you call me when you get to the wedding dress shop and then when you're on your way home? I worry about you and the baby."

She'd gone around the world multiple times, lived in war zones and refugee camps for months on end, and no one had worried about her. Jean-Claude had left her without so much as a backward glance in rebel-infested villages for weeks sometimes, with only a promise to return as soon as he could. And here Erik was stressing about an hour-and-a-half trip into Winnipeg. Her heart softened a little more. Maybe she should tell him.

No, she had to keep some things to herself, at least until she knew this marriage was for more than just expediency.

"If that will make you happy." She stretched up on tiptoe and replaced her thumb with her lips, pulling back before he could deepen the kiss and destroy her resolve.

"Coming with you would make me happy. This will just let me breathe while you're gone."

"Really, Erik. I've been in much more serious situations. I can look after myself." She drowned the burgeoning hope that he truly cared for her under a deluge of self-reproach. This was only a temporary arrangement, and she needed to be able to stand on her own once it was over.

"I know. But now you don't have to. I'm here to care for you—you and the baby."

It was a nice sentiment; however, she could see this smothering was going to get old very fast. "Erik, if this relationship is going to work, you have to give me some space. I'm not used to all this … this…"

"Loving?" he provided as his grandmother entered the room with papers clutched in her arthritic hand.

"Yes, loving." She kissed him again quickly, for his grandmother's sake. The fact that she felt the gentle touch at the ends of her toes meant nothing. "Now go help your gran and mom plan the happiest day of our lives."

She fled from the house as though it were full of Afghani militants.

A spurt of gravel accompanied her departure from the farmyard. She turned onto the highway, jacked up the tunes, and savored her first taste of freedom in more than two weeks. Get in, get out, and don't be seen had turned into get engaged, discover pregnancy, and get married. There wasn't much further her plan could have deteriorated in such a short time.

As she tried on her wedding dress, she shut her mind to all the issues and complications and just reveled in the knowledge that tomorrow she was marrying a good man she enjoyed being with.

Three hours later, she parked the SUV and went the rest of the way on foot. She hadn't expected The Forks to be so busy on a weekday, even though it was summer. Glancing around, she was amazed at the crowds. Oh well. The Yemeni contact had told her to pick someplace public. She hoped he could find her among all the people.

Analise wandered around the market and then sat on a bench with a decaf iced coffee to listen to a singing group that had set up in the bandstand. It sounded as though they were practicing for a performance on the weekend, as one of the group kept stopping the song to say a few things and then made them begin again. When she heard the start of "Hey Jude" for the fourth time, she was about to get up and walk away, until a dark-haired man sat next to her.

Instantly, she stiffened, suppressing a shudder. He

smelled of cigarette smoke and coffee breath. Although dressed in jeans and a dark blue T-shirt, he didn't seem local. She didn't dare turn to see his face, didn't want to bring back any unwelcome memories. Jean-Claude hadn't often introduced her to his contacts, and now she knew why. But the few she had met had made her feel uneasy. How could she not have listened to her instinct telling her there was something wrong? Maybe then she wouldn't be in this mess.

"They should practice at home and not here in public," the man said softly, his thick Arab accent sending a shiver up her spine.

"Yes, but they want to get it right on the night. So I guess practicing at the venue gives them a real sense of what it will be like to perform," she replied.

"J-C said you were too nice. I am sorry he is gone. You can trust that his death has been avenged."

This time, she didn't try to hold back the shudder. "There has been too much death. I hope it's over."

"You are out of it now. Stay away from the Middle East for a while. Your treatment by the French government was five stars compared with the way the other side will try to extract information from you."

"I have no intention of returning. And I have no information to give. I didn't even know Jean-Claude was in that business."

"Yes, he did his best to keep it from you. He loved you. We told him to leave you; it wasn't safe for him to have a woman. Yet he was always so confident, saying he could protect you."

Yes, that sounded like her dead fiancé. Still, his

deception hurt. *Had she ever really known him?*

"That was Jean-Claude." An errant tear slipped down her cheek, and she angrily wiped it away. Others had seen the danger she was in, but to him, his own pleasure was more important.

"He left this for you." The man slid a bag between them. As she moved to peer into it, his hand came over hers, squeezing painfully. "Not here. I have broken protocol enough by speaking with you. I was to drop the bag and go. There is more in a Cayman Islands bank account, but try not to touch that for a year or two, in case the account is being watched."

"If it's blood money, I don't want it," she protested.

"The only blood on this money is Jean-Claude's. It belongs to you; you deserve it. Be happy and forget about him." With that pronouncement, the man stood and walked away, melting into the crowd in seconds. If it weren't for the stiff leather satchel next to her, she'd have wondered if she'd dreamed the whole exchange.

Hoisting the bag's strap onto her shoulder, she picked up her shopping and returned to the SUV, remembering to call Erik to tell him she was on her way home. The satchel sat on the passenger seat, mocking her cowardice. When she was miles out of town and the highway was deserted, she pulled over to see what Jean-Claude had left her.

Inside the bag were ten bundles of used American bills. She undid one of the rolls and counted up to $50,000. There were also some gold coins and a bag of precious gems. What did Jean-Claude think she was, some kind of mastermind criminal to monetize this lot? The pawn shop had been suspicious enough when she'd gone to hawk her diamond ring. She'd made up some lame story about the stone belonging to her mother who had once been engaged to a man from Africa. Thinking back, Jean-Claude had given it to her right after he'd returned from a solitary visit to the Congo, an area known for its trade in conflict diamonds. Was everything he'd given her tainted with blood?

Except the baby.

For the sake of their child, she'd remember the good things about her former fiancé. Tell the baby the best about his or her father—his quirky sense of humor and his fascination with flamingoes. She had loved Jean-Claude. He'd kept her from being alone and held her when she was sad. But it wasn't the deep, emotional pull she felt toward Erik. In a way, her former fiancé had led her back to her first love. He'd probably have laughed at the irony of that.

She shoved the money, jewels, and coins back into the bag. A black leather booklet was in an inside zip pocket. There was a list of account numbers with figures scribbled in Jean-Claude's backward Arabic. If what she read was true, she was now a very wealthy woman.

She could pay back Erik, buy herself a nice house in the south of France, and raise her baby without having to worry about work or money. Question was, would she?

Putting the SUV back in gear, she merged onto the

empty highway, heading back to her grandfather's place. She now had a way out. Could she leave Erik at the altar to face the mess her departure would leave behind?

Or was it time she stopped running?

***

"Well, thanks for calling." Erik hung up and scrubbed his hands over his face. He didn't know which was worse—his gossiping, busybody family or the constant worry that Analise was one click of the heels away from leaving again.

Who had Analise met with in Winnipeg? Was Jean-Claude really dead? It was clear the girl he used to know had morphed into a woman with secrets. Could he trust her? The only way to find out was to go straight to the source.

"Everything all right, son?" His grandfather plodded into the kitchen, the rubber tip of his cane making a squeaking noise on the linoleum.

"Yeah. Aunt Gemma just called to say she was coming to the wedding tomorrow. I need to get out of here for a while. Think you can cover for me while I escape out the back door?"

"Absolutely. And, Erik?"

"Yes, Gramps?"

"Don't believe everything you hear. Go with your gut."

Erik stared. How much had he heard? But his advice was sound. His gut told him Analise was a wounded bird that, once healed, would stay true to her nest. He snuck out the back door as he heard his mother call his name. His grandfather winked at him and shot a salute. Always helped to have ex-Army at your back.

Relief swept through him when he saw Analise's silver SUV parked in front of the stables. Was he going to feel this way every time he came home? *Yay, she hasn't left me today*. That wasn't going to work for either of them. They had to talk.

There was no answer at the house, so he wandered around to the barns out back. As he approached the old wooden structure, Analise's voice stopped him in his tracks.

"I've got the money now, *Afi*. You can get whatever you want, or go wherever you want. Are you sure you want to start up here again? We could get a small place in England, Ireland, or even Iceland. It would be just the three of us."

His stomach fell. She was leaving. But not before he got an explanation.

"What about Erik?" Gunnar asked.

"Yes, what about Erik?" He stepped into the barn.

Analise jumped before whirling around. "Oh, Erik. I wasn't expecting you."

"I figured that. Planning on skipping out on the wedding? Leaving me at the altar in front of my entire family?" He couldn't help the bitterness of his tone. She'd just taken a hatchet to his heart.

"I think you two lovebirds need to talk. I'm going to have a quick wash and head to Rosie's for dinner," Gunnar said in the deafening silence.

"Are you going to answer my questions?" Erik demanded after the older man left the barn.

Analise took a deep breath, and for a moment he didn't think she was going to say anything. Then she crossed her arms, her feet planted hip-width apart. "Erik, this is all so sudden for me. I picked up my wedding dress today. My wedding dress! Two weeks ago I drove into town to see my grandfather, get him to come on holiday to Iceland, and then return to my career. I had no plans to get engaged, much less married. I'm freaking out."

"This wasn't on my vacation agenda either. I know, though, that we can make this work. But first, you have to trust me."

He stood his ground. She needed to come to him for once. Needed to choose him over running away. He opened his arms. She hesitated only a minute before she stepped forward and nestled against his chest. *Home.* The word flitted through his mind. Didn't matter if it was Akureyri, London, or Paris. As long as she was in his arms, he was home.

Analise's sigh went straight through his shirt and warmed his chest. Was it an expression of surrender or realization that this was where she should be? After a moment, she raised her face. Her fingers threaded into his hair and brought his lips down to hers. Their previous kisses had started gentle, building in heat. This one was molten from the start, searing his mind of all rational thought.

He stumbled back until he hit a pile of straw. It'd been many years since he'd literally had a roll in the hay. It was a lot itchier than he remembered. When Analise's small hand found the hem of his shirt and ventured underneath to caress his back, he forgot the discomfort and concentrated on her taste, the feel of her in his arms, the softness of her skin. He wasn't quite sure when his shirt disappeared, but he was very aware when his pants became too tight. His hand had found its way under her top, and with one flick, her bra was undone. He wedged one hand between their bodies so he could feel the bounty now bared to him. Analise's moan of pleasure fueled his desire. That was one engine that wasn't going to run dry.

He shifted to access more of her body, and a sharp shaft of straw speared into his back. Reluctantly, he pulled his mouth from Analise's and forced his hands to return to her hips. His chest heaved as he tried to regain his normal breathing, and his heartbeat pounded in his ears. "I'm not a teenager anymore. We need someplace more comfortable." His voice was husky with desire.

She scrambled to her feet. Her chest rose and fell rapidly, and a flush was on every part of skin he could see. Her bra was askew, and her nipples were clearly outlined against her top, taunting him. Why had he stopped? *Idiot.*

He followed her up, and when she didn't move, he stared into her eyes. "Is it okay, with the baby, I mean?" In the passion of the moment he'd forgotten entirely that she was pregnant. Forgotten everything, in fact, except how much he wanted her. She was potent. He'd even forgotten about the man she'd met in

Winnipeg.

"The baby's okay. But…"

He could see a battle going on inside her, and his own guts clenched. Was she conflicted about making love with him or was something else upsetting her? The one thing he did know was that now was the time to find out. There would be another opportunity, he hoped, to take her to bed. Unless he mucked this up now.

"Let's talk. I think we have some issues to resolve before tomorrow." He found his T-shirt and tugged it on while she straightened her clothes. She took his hand, and they went back to the house without saying anything.

"Sit here; I'll get us something to drink," he said as they stepped onto the porch.

He returned a few minutes later with two glasses of cold lemonade. There were several pieces of straw in her hair and a couple on her shirt. He plucked them off after handing her the glass. Taking a long drink, hoping to cool the lingering heat in his groin, he leaned against the railing in front of her.

"Okay, you start," he said. Because he sure as hell had no idea where to begin.

She hesitated, then took a deep breath. "We can't keep doing this."

"Doing what?" His brain was still back in the barn.

"Kissing when we need to talk. Jean-Claude always used sex to get what he wanted. Whenever I disagreed with him, he'd start kissing me until I agreed to do as he asked. Then afterward I'd hate myself for my weakness. If we're going to have any kind of future together, even if it's a short one, you can't take advantage of my … passion." She stared at the floor during her whole speech.

He waited for her to look at him. "I'm sorry. I wasn't trying to manipulate you. I can honestly say that I had absolutely no ulterior motive. I kissed you because I wanted to kiss you and I was pretty sure you wanted to be kissed. You might have noticed we have explosive chemistry. If I'm making love to you, my singular motive is to bring you pleasure and bring us closer."

"I thought you said this marriage was going to be in name only," she reminded him.

Busted.

"I'll leave that up to you. If there's any point in this marriage when you want to change that clause then I'm open to renegotiation. However, there is one thing that is nonnegotiable. If this relationship is going to work, even on the most basic level, we have to be honest with each other."

"Yes."

"Who did you meet today?"

She dropped her glass and watched as it rolled to a stop against the post for the handrail, spreading a trail of liquid as it went.

She leapt to her feet, her head swiveling from right to left as though mentally mapping all the possible escape routes. "How do you know about that? Did you follow me?"

"No, I didn't. Unfortunately, I have relatives

everywhere. One of my aunts saw you at The Forks."

Wringing her hands, she paced the porch. As she passed him, he reached out and grabbed her arm. "Was it Jean-Claude?" He ground the name out through the bile that rose up in his mouth.

"No, absolutely not. Jean-Claude is dead. I guess, in the spirit of honesty, I should tell you a little more about him."

Erik wasn't sure he wanted to hear more about a sexy Frenchman who could turn a determined Analise from her way with his kisses. "Go on."

"Jean-Claude was a spy."

"What?"

"I didn't know about it until he died. Remember I said I was injured and woke up in hospital? What I didn't tell you was that hospital was in Algeria. I was kept in detention for weeks while they grilled me about what I knew of his activities, who he'd been meeting with, where, demanding any photos I'd taken of him with his contacts…"

"And you never knew?" *Great, she was in love with James Bond.* How was a guy supposed to compete with a dead spy?

"In hindsight, it's all so clear—the clandestine meetings, the coded messages. As an exceptional freelance journalist, this was normal. To get the real story you had to dig deep, meet with people who knew what was happening. And they usually weren't governmental authorities. But while we were together, I had no idea."

"Why did the French government question you?

Shouldn't they have known who he was meeting already?"

Analise took a deep breath, as though what she was going to say was a betrayal. "It seems there was some question over whom exactly he worked for. Not all of his reports went to the French secret service."

"So, who did you meet this afternoon?" Could Analise have taken the vacant position left by her fiancé?

"I found a message from Jean-Claude. It directed me to contact a certain number. They set up a meeting, which happened today."

Erik fought down his anger. How was he supposed to keep her safe if she went off and met strange spies without him? He stared at the woman opposite him who had dropped once more into her grandmother's rocking chair. She looked so similar to ten years ago, minus the long hair, that he was having a difficult time remembering that she was now a grown woman who'd led an adventurous life without him. He needed to get to know this enigma who had fascinated him from the moment she'd rolled down her window on the highway.

However, her association with the world of espionage held other complications. As a mergers and acquisitions lawyer, he needed to keep his reputation squeaky clean. Affiliation with the underside of the world, especially any possible terrorist connections, would be the death knell to his career. He might have been giving up the London partnership, but he wasn't finished with being a lawyer. Analise was playing with fire, and if he stayed with her he could get burned—badly.

Some of what he was thinking must have shown on his face.

"Now that you know my sordid past, I understand completely if you want to call off the wedding tomorrow. Granddad and I can manage. I've weathered gossip before. I can do it again."

Her simple statement, spoken with a flat, lifeless voice, cut through all the questions floating around in his head. He wanted this woman. He needed this woman. "What ifs" weren't going to get in the way of what could be the most important decision in his life.

"I told you once before. You will never be alone again. I asked you to marry me. I'm not taking that back because your ex played loosey-goosey with world politics."

Her radiant smile was stunning. Before he got distracted again, there was still the issue of her desire to run away with her grandfather.

"Where did you suddenly get the money to leave?"

"The French government has frozen all my assets, but Jean-Claude left money, some jewels and gold coins, and details about a supposed secret bank account with the man I met. That's why I could offer my grandfather a way out. And now I have the money to pay you back."

"I don't want your money," he reminded her. Or, more precisely, he didn't want Jean-Claude's money. "However, I do want your word."

"My word?"

"That you'll show up tomorrow and make an honest man out of me. My grandparents would never recover if their grandson was left at the altar."

She stood and put her hands on his shoulders, standing on tiptoe to give him an all-too-brief kiss on the lips. "I like your grandparents."

"What about me?"

"I like you too," she whispered. Then she pulled back and strode toward the door. "As tomorrow is my wedding day, I guess I'd better get some rest. Can't be looking tired and worn out with all your relatives staring at me."

And with that, she was gone. Was it his imagination or did the screen door slamming sound like prison bars sliding closed? Despite the intense summer heat, he shivered.

Chapter Thirteen

She shifted from one foot to the other, fiddling with her bouquet.

"Stand still, Analise. I can't get this headdress right if you keep fidgeting. It's hard enough getting it to stay in your short hair." Tracy jammed a couple more pins into her head before giving the whole thing a liberal spraying with what surely must have been hair cement.

"Sorry. I didn't expect to get married so soon or I wouldn't have cut my hair short."

Tracy moved to stand in front, her critical eye surveying her handiwork. "And I bet you didn't expect Erik's grandmother to insist that you wear her fifty-pound veil, either. Still, wear it up the aisle to make her happy, then we can ditch it later for the reception."

"Thank God. I think my neck is going to snap. They sure made brides a lot stronger in the old days."

"Well, if it's any consolation, they didn't make them any more beautiful. I can't believe you got that dress in less than a week. It's absolutely gorgeous."

Tracy moved to the side, and Analise surveyed herself in the full-length mirror. She'd been so glad when Tracy had offered to help her get ready. If it had been left to her and her grandfather, she'd have had half the million buttons down the back undone. Roving her critical photographer eye over the woman in the mirror, she gave a slight nod of acceptance. The dress did look nice, and the flowers picked this morning from Erik's grandmother's garden were bright and cheery and full of gorgeous perfume. She took a deep breath near the lavender, hoping the calming scent would soothe the butterflies fluttering in her belly.

Still staring at her reflection, Analise had to clear her throat before she could talk. "Tracy, how did you feel on your wedding day?"

"Excited, nervous, terrified. All the way up the aisle I thought I was going to vomit. Then, when I saw Brent standing there, looking like he'd just won the lottery, all of a sudden it made sense. The rest of the day was one of the happiest of my life, only eclipsed by the days our children were born."

Analise smiled. Would seeing Erik have the same curative powers, or would the doubts that had plagued her all night long come back twofold? She'd promised not to leave him at the altar, but she couldn't guarantee she wouldn't bolt as soon as the minister asked if anyone had a reason why the marriage shouldn't take place.

Excuse me, but I can't actually marry this man because I think I might be falling in love with him again, and if this ends badly I may not be able to put the pieces back together this time.

A tentative knock on the door made Tracy scurry to answer the summons. Analise held her breath; she didn't know if she could handle more interference from Erik's mother. Her soon-to-be mother-in-law had already been to the small dressing room three times in the last forty minutes. Thankfully, Tracy had managed to get her to leave within five minutes of each invasion. Analise prepared herself for whatever Susan Sigurdson could suggest next. Because if it were any more ridiculous baby names, Analise would run screaming from the building. Primrose if it was a girl? Really?

Instead, standing at the door was her grandfather, resplendent in a three-piece suit, a red rose, and a spray of baby's breath in his buttonhole. His silver hair had been brushed back off his face, and his cheeks were freshly shaven. He was a little older but once again looked the vibrant man who had hugged her till she couldn't breathe as a teenager.

"You're beautiful, sweet. Are you ready?"

"Ready as I'll ever be, *Afi*."

Tracy followed behind, bundling the long veil so Analise could walk without her head being pulled backward by the weight. As they approached the doors to the ballroom where the ceremony and the reception were to be held, her grandfather paused.

"Are you sure about this?" His voice was gruff with emotion.

Analise put her arms around him, tucking her head under his chin as she'd done all those years ago. His heartbeat was strong, and the arms that wrapped around her back held her tightly. She gave him one final squeeze before pulling back.

"I'm sure. Erik is a good, caring man. He'll look after me almost as well as you."

"He better," *Afi* declared.

The music began, and she was walking up the aisle on her grandfather's arm. As she neared, her eyes met Erik's. He didn't quite look like he'd won the lottery, but pretty close. They could make this work. All was right with her life, if only for one brief moment.

***

Analise wasn't sure which hurt more, her cheeks or her feet. The new heels pinched her big toe until it throbbed. She alternated slipping her shoes off each foot until she wasn't sure if she would ever be able to get the footwear back on again. The photographer, although nice, had insisted on taking 600 shots of her and Erik with endless variations of family in the background. Next time she married, it would be to a man with fewer relatives.

"How are you holding up?" Erik asked as the photographer went off to find another memory card or download some of the photos onto her laptop.

"My feet are killing me, my cheeks may never be the same again, and if one more person asks if I can feel the baby yet, I'll give them a kick," she said through a smile.

Erik caressed her face. "If it's any consolation, you're doing a fabulous job. My grandmother and mother are in tears."

"And that's a good thing?"

"Yes, they're tears of joy. Trust me, if they weren't happy, I'd have heard about it. And have you noticed? Mom has stayed sober."

"I did notice. I'm glad she's hopefully getting better." Analise looked around at the crowd. "Weddings aren't really for the bride and groom, are they?" The room had been transformed from wedding chapel to reception banquet hall in the hour they'd been outside taking photos.

"No, that's what honeymoons are for. Speaking of which, I've booked us a room at the Hecla Island Resort for tonight and tomorrow night, and then from next Friday we've got two weeks in the Seychelles to truly relax."

"Sounds heavenly." She sighed. The thought of two weeks in the sun with nothing to do except read and get to know Erik was just what she needed to make it through the rest of the evening.

Erik put his arm around her waist, and they strolled over to where Brent and Tracy were conversing with another couple around the same age. Analise smiled and nodded, hoping her nods were in time with the general conversation. She let the words buzz over her, already trying to picture herself lying on the beach, Erik's strong fingers working out a particularly stubborn knot in her neck muscles. As she was imagining his hands moving from her neck down to her back to untie her bikini top, she felt him stiffen next to her. His hand at her waist tensed.

She glanced up at her new husband to see him staring at the doorway, a scowl on his face. Despite the endless parade of relatives, a few of whom she knew he didn't particularly care for, he'd never once showed anything but a welcoming smile. Who could elicit such a negative response from Erik?

"What the hell is she doing here?" he muttered. "Excuse me," he said to the group before striding over to the door.

"Who's that?" Brent asked. The woman had a huge smile on her face as she saw Erik advancing toward her. But rather than welcoming her to the party, Erik grabbed her arm and steered her out the door before anyone could blink.

"She's not a relative?" Analise glanced around the room to see if anyone else had noticed the odd behavior. Everyone seemed engrossed in their own conversations, waiting for the call to dinner.

"I've never seen her before," Brent replied. "Erik didn't seem too happy to see her."

Should she follow her husband, or should she stay and wait for him to return and explain? Trust was the cornerstone of any solid relationship. But the possessive way the unknown woman had looked at Erik made the hairs on the back of Analise's neck stand on end.

"Analise, where's Erik? We want to get started on the supper and need him to announce it and ask everyone to sit down," her new mother-in-law said.

Just the excuse she needed.

"I'll go find him. I think he stepped out for a minute. Maybe Brent could make the announcement; we'll be back to sit at the head table in a minute."

Erik's mother ambled toward the front table while Brent eyed the microphone with distaste. "I hate talking into those things," he said, then went to do as he was asked.

Analise headed for the door, having to pause several times while Erik's relatives commented on her dress or the simple ceremony that had made them man and wife. Finally free, she wandered down the corridor, curious as to what Erik could need to discuss so urgently with this woman that he'd leave their wedding reception. As she approached the corner near the kitchen, she heard Erik's low tones followed by a woman's higher-pitched one. Although she couldn't quite make out what they were saying, the woman seemed distressed, and Erik was trying to soothe her.

Analise took another couple of steps closer, not sure whether she should interrupt or not, as they were obviously having a private conversation. As she was about to round the corner, she heard Erik distinctly say, "Brenda, listen to me. It's a marriage of convenience. Analise is pregnant, and I'm helping her out so that she's not ostracized from the community. I wasn't carrying on with her while we were together. I've known her for ten years. She was my sister's best friend. We pretended to be engaged when we first arrived to get my mother off my back about getting married, and things escalated from there."

Analise leaned against the wall, out of sight. The woman was Erik's ex-girlfriend, who obviously wanted him back. Too bad she hadn't arrived a couple of hours ago; she could have saved them all a lot of heartache. Although he'd never said the words, she'd assumed Erik cared for more than just her reputation. She didn't wait to hear Brenda's rebuttal. She fled to the bathroom and threw up.

***

Erik escorted Brenda to her rental car, checking over his shoulder to see if anyone had seen him. Of all the terrible timings, she would have to show up now. She'd probably thought he'd reconsider ending their relationship when surrounded by his family.

The only thing that had calmed her down after she learned this was his wedding and "someone had stolen her man" was the news that it was a marriage of convenience. He hoped by the time Brenda worked out that he intended to stay married for life, she'd already have found someone else.

As the taillights of her rental car disappeared, Erik strolled back into the reception hall. Brenda's unexpected arrival aside, the day had gone brilliantly. Analise had looked so beautiful as she held his hand in front of the minister. The fragile, vulnerable look had disappeared from her eyes, and she finally seemed ready to blossom. Even the nausea that had plagued her for the past week seemed to have passed.

Entering the dining room, he was surprised to see two empty spots at the head table. The rest of the guests were already seated, and the wait staff was busy serving the first course. His mother waved to him frantically. Ignoring her, he made his way over to Brent.

"Where's Analise?" he tried to ask nonchalantly, but a hint of panic entered his voice.

"She went to find you. Thought maybe you two were having a little pre-wedding night cuddle in the corridor."

"She's probably freshening up in the ladies' room. I'll go check," Tracy offered.

Erik did his best to quell the sense of impending disaster that made his stomach sink to his knees. Could Analise have overheard him trying to calm Brenda?

His mother was still waving at him, so he wandered over to the head table as though nothing were amiss. His grandparents were tucking into their salads, oblivious to the fact that one of the central figures of the day was missing. He took his seat and toyed with his food as he kept his eyes riveted on the door. After what seemed an eternity, Analise finally returned with Tracy.

He tried to tell if she was upset or had simply been freshening up. She wore the glacial mask that she'd had on so frequently during her first week in Manitoba. The look that said while her body was here, her mind and spirit were on some tropical island having a much better time. He knew it was a coping mechanism she employed to distance herself from the trauma of her work. It did not bode well for him that she was behaving that way now.

As she approached, she plastered a smile on her lips that didn't reach her eyes. She stopped and kissed both his grandparents on the cheek, wishing them a wonderful anniversary before taking the seat next to him.

"Are you okay?"

"Fine," was her monosyllabic reply. Which, of course, meant the exact opposite.

For the rest of the evening Analise played the part of blushing bride to perfection. They danced the first dance with his grandparents sharing the floor. Each couple cut a cake, wedding or anniversary. He was sure if he asked any of the attendees, they'd have said that both couples were spectacularly in love and that sixty-five years from now they'd be celebrating another anniversary.

Only Erik, aware of how tightly Analise was holding herself, of the vacant aspect of her smile, knew all was not rosy at the head table.

***

Analise stepped into the tiny hotel room and flung herself on the bed. *What the hell is wrong with me? Will I never learn? I let myself get lost in the romance again. Forgot it's all for show.* Hearing Erik tell his ex-girlfriend that the marriage meant nothing to him hurt beyond belief. It wasn't as if the news was new to her. But to hear him explain the reasons for their marriage had shattered every illusion she'd built up over the past five days. Once again, her world had come crashing down. Only by channeling all her inner focus had she been able to see the evening through without running screaming from the banquet hall.

The hour drive up to Hecla had been conducted in complete silence. Erik had concentrated on the dark road, darting worried glances in her direction, obviously not knowing how to broach the subject that loomed between them.

The *click* of the door heralded his arrival in the room. She rolled over on the bed and stared at her husband. In all her girlhood dreams, this was not how she had imagined her wedding night. Although, Erik, in his perfectly fitted suit, certainly fit the bill of a dream man. Too bad it was all just a fantasy.

He leaned against the door, not advancing into the room. Had he arranged to meet Brenda here? Was he just going to explain and then head down the hall to her? Perhaps seeing his ex-girlfriend again had reminded him of all they had in common—of how much easier their lives would mesh together. Analise clutched her stomach, willing her dinner to stay inside.

"Are you feeling sick?" He was at her side in an instant. "Can I get you some water? A cool washcloth? Is your leg bothering you?"

She leveraged herself up, glad Tracy had helped her change out of her wedding dress before they'd left. Wearing a tailored pantsuit, it was much easier to flee to the bathroom should she need to vomit.

"My leg is fine. I'm fine."

"You keep saying that when you're obviously not. You heard me talking to Brenda, didn't you?"

"Yes. But honestly, Erik, it's no big deal. We both know this marriage is a sham, like our engagement. We don't even need to wait till the baby is born. In a month or so we can cite irreconcilable differences, and then you can go back to Brenda. I hope she understood and is willing to wait. Of course, if you want to see her in the meantime…"

Erik knelt on the floor and took her hand in his. "Listen, I said those things to her so she wouldn't make a scene. Can you imagine the questions if she announced that less than a month ago she was my girlfriend? I didn't want our wedding day, or my grandparents' anniversary party, to be tainted by her tantrum. I have absolutely no intention of ever seeing her again, much less getting back together with her."

He said it with such sincerity that she believed him. He'd asked her to trust him. This seemed a good time to start. Plus, she was the one with both his rings on her finger. She'd prove she was the right woman for him. But not tonight. She was too tired.

"*Je suis bien fatiguée*. I'm exhausted. Do you mind if I go to bed now?"

A flicker of passion blazed in his eyes until she yawned. "Of course. Are you sure you don't want something to eat? I was reading about morning sickness, and it said that eating small meals more frequently often helps. I could order some toast and tea for you from room service."

"Toast and tea? You've been living with the British too long. I'll have to indoctrinate you in the ways of the French. We'll start tomorrow. Tonight, I just need to sleep."

"If you're the teacher, I look forward to French class." His voice dropped, and the sexy way he glanced at her prone body made her reconsider her need for rest. Didn't they say you got the best sleep after relieving your body of all tension? Before she could suggest he join her on the bed, another yawn contorted her face. *Zut*, by the time he had his shoes off she'd likely be asleep. Exploring his body would have to wait until tomorrow.

When she returned from the bathroom, Erik was trying to get comfortable in one of the bucket chairs. "I checked with reception, and they're all full up, so I can't get another room," he explained.

"Get in the bed, Erik. I'm going to be out like a light in two minutes anyway. I won't know if you're next to me or in another room. I should warn you, though, I roll a lot when I sleep. So if you wake up, and I'm on top of you, just push me off."

"No way, no how am I going to push my gorgeous wife off me in bed. And in the spirit of honesty, I should warn you that I didn't pack pajamas."

Mon Dieu.

Chapter Fourteen

Erik woke with Analise's head on his chest, her hand on his heart, and her thigh flung across his midriff. He inhaled deeply, trying to calm that part of his anatomy that was reacting predictably. She'd warned him that she moved a lot in the bed; what she hadn't told him was that she did so while wearing very little.

When she'd emerged from the bathroom last night all she'd had on was a tiny baby-doll nightie that, for the most part, was see-through. He'd then spent ten minutes under a freezing cold shower reminding himself of all the reasons why he couldn't make love to his bride on their wedding night. Thankfully, as she'd predicted, she'd been fast asleep by the time he came to bed.

His only hope now was to ease out of bed before she woke. Despite the passionate kisses they'd shared, Analise hadn't definitively said she wanted to consummate their marriage. And he needed to tread carefully. Their merger was at a critical stage, and if he wanted to make it permanent, then a little restraint now was needed. Analise had to make the first move. Already, though, it was his body in motion. He had to get out of bed while he still could.

Should he try the infamous *Friends* hug and roll maneuver? As he prepared to exit with his libido under control, Analise moved. Her hand slid down to his groin, cupping his erection, which grew even larger under her fingers. *Oh God!* He suppressed a groan and tried to shift sideways so both her hand and leg harmlessly fell away to the mattress.

The pattern of her breathing changed. She was about to wake. With one last, desperate attempt to extricate his body before he embarrassed himself, he rolled her over with a swift move. Before he could roll back her eyes flew open. Confusion clouded her gaze for a moment as she saw him hovering above her, then a smile lit her face like sunshine on a ripe wheat field.

"*Bonjour.* I take it I was all over you." Her morning voice was so sexy Erik had to clench his teeth together before responding.

"I'm not complaining, but I'd better get up now." For God's sake, if she wriggled once more underneath him, neither of them would be moving from this bed for hours, maybe days.

"Wait." The pressure of her hand on his back was so slight he could have moved with very little effort. Yet its effect was as though a car sat on top of him.

"Yes?" He raised an eyebrow; the ridiculousness of the situation made him want to laugh. He had to be the first bridegroom in history to try to make a quick exit out of his marriage bed.

"You asked on Friday what I wanted for a wedding present. I know now."

Please say for me to make love to you, please, please.

"And what would that be?" Either rigor mortis had

set in early or every muscle in his body was paralyzed, awaiting her next words.

"I want to go back in time, just for one day."

Erik searched her eyes. Maybe she was still asleep? Was she talking in a dream?

"Umm, I don't understand," he replied.

"I want to pretend the past ten years haven't happened. I want to imagine what it would be like if Karen hadn't died, if I hadn't left and met that other guy." He was grateful she hadn't mentioned her dead lover's name while in bed with him.

"Sounds wonderful. Where do you want to start?"

"Right here. Let's pretend it's the morning after graduation. Do you remember we had secret plans to spend the night together? Imagine that I fell asleep on you, as I did last night, and we're waking to a new day, in bed together. The magic ends at midnight, so make the most of it, Prairie Boy."

"You know what you're asking, don't you? Even ten years ago I was consumed with lust for you. You really want me to make love to you?"

She nodded. "Like it's my first time," she whispered.

Damn.

That might call for more restraint than he could muster at the moment. Yet, for her, he was going to make a valiant effort. He was already rock-hard; it was going to take every ounce of his self-control to make this last more than ten minutes.

She closed her eyes and parted her lips. He touched them softly with his own, tasting her sweetness, her innocence, her vulnerability. If it killed him, he was going to make this the best lovemaking session she'd ever known.

An hour later, he stared at the ceiling, unable to control the huge smile that covered his face. Analise lay in the same position as when he'd awakened this morning, only this time, there weren't even the scraps of cloth between them. Her baby-doll nightie, her wedding present to him, was somewhere behind the dresser. Her warmth melted the last of his resistance. There was nothing, nothing he'd let separate them again.

"Wow," she said, her breath cool against his overheated skin. Her index finger was drawing hearts in the smattering of hair on his chest.

"Not bad for a first time." One hand ran up and down her back as though it still couldn't get enough of touching her. The other was toying with a small lock of her hair.

She levered herself up on an elbow and stared him in the eye. "You think you can improve on that?"

Her face free of makeup, the glow of loving still on her skin, he could almost believe they'd turned back the clock. The brazen way she ran her inner thigh up over his groin, which was stirring to life again, reminded him, however, that she was no longer a girl—she was all woman.

"Is that a challenge?" he wheezed out on an involuntary exhalation.

Her hand that had been tracing patterns on his chest slipped lower, over his abdomen. "Well, I'm a more experienced lover now. Let's see how you handle that."

Her hand slipped over his hip before crossing his upper thigh to slide between his legs.

Game on.

***

Analise shifted in the passenger seat of Erik's BMW. The top was down, and a cool breeze blew through her hair. They'd spent twenty of the past twenty-four hours in bed, and she'd never felt so wonderful in her life. She now knew the difference between sex and lovemaking. They were worlds apart, and she didn't ever want to go back to the former. Erik never made her feel used, only cherished. Even during their most passionate encounters he'd always made sure she was satisfied first. And she'd used every trick she knew to try to crack his self-control.

"Where are we going?" It wasn't until they were approaching Akureyri that she questioned their ultimate destination. Would they be staying at one of their grandparents' places? That would be awkward, given how loud they'd been in bed together. It also dawned on her how much control she'd already given to Erik, allowing him to make decisions about her future. This trust thing was going to take some getting used to. In the meantime, they'd better work on their communication.

"To your grandfather's place first. He's offered us the house until we sort out where we're going to live."

"Where's *Afi* going?" She couldn't imagine making love to Erik in her old room while her grandfather listened to the bed creaking through the thin wall. Heat invaded her face at the thought.

"He's borrowed a trailer and was going to move it onto the property while we were up in Hecla. I offered for us to stay in the trailer, but he insisted. He said a new married couple needed some space and breathing room, without an old man in earshot."

Analise raised her face to the wind, hoping the rushing air cooled the blush she knew was staining her cheeks bright red. Obviously it didn't work too well as Erik glanced over at her and laughed.

"I hope you don't mind. I thought you'd like it better than staying at my grandparents' farm." Erik shuddered. "I can picture my mother knocking on the door every ten minutes asking if we're coming out for breakfast."

"Definitely. I guess we should discuss where we're going to spend the next year or so. Don't you have to go back to London?"

"Only to resign. The merger's done, but there might be a few bits of paper to sort out. Once that's complete, then I'm a free agent and can move where I want. If you want to live in London, they've offered me a permanent position. My French is pretty appalling, so I don't think I'd be much good in France. However, if that's where you prefer, I'm happy to give it a try and figure something out."

"Really?" Jean-Claude had never asked her opinion about where they were going to go next. He'd always just told her. Erik was definitely more of a man than the former spy.

"Really. I've run roughshod over you enough the past two weeks. This is supposed to be a partnership. Of course you get a say in where we'll live."

They pulled into her grandfather's driveway. "Here. I want to live here." The certainty hit her as they bumped along the gravel path. This was the one place she'd considered a real home. A place where love and friendship blossomed like the climbing rose that covered the trellis over the porch. It weathered the hard times and grew stronger with each year. It was the best place to raise her baby.

Erik pulled the car to a stop and put his hand over hers in her lap. "I was hoping you'd say that. I think it's time I came home as well."

She searched his face. Wasn't this supposed to be a short-term arrangement? He sounded as though he was talking about forever. Maybe this marriage had more life in it than she'd expected.

"I do have to go back to Paris in six weeks. There's going to be an exhibition of my work at the Hôtel de Ville. I promised to make a personal appearance. But the show is only scheduled for two weeks. And I need to clear my name with the French government. I don't want my passport flagged forever. Maybe you could help with that."

"Absolutely. How 'bout this for a plan: we'll head to Europe after our honeymoon in the Seychelles. First stop, London, to clear out my things, then Paris to sort out yours. We can move here in time for a cozy winter

holed up in a little house till we can build our own."
Erik shut the trunk after he removed their overnight
bags.

"Sounds perfect." She could've flown to the
neighboring farm she was so lighthearted. She loved
Erik. She could feel it in her bones. It was so different
from what she'd felt for Jean-Claude.

This was friendship and partnership and desire all
melded into such a hope for the future she couldn't stop
smiling.

Even the familiar farmyard looked like heaven to
her. An old trailer was parked next to the barn, a bright
yellow extension cord running into the stables. Her
grandfather appeared in the doorway as she stepped
onto the porch.

"Oh, you're back," he called out to them.
"Welcome home!"

"Go say hi to your granddad, my love. I'll put our
bags in the house."

She gave him a quick kiss on the cheek. Finally,
everything was going right in her world. A few months
of this happiness, and she'd soon be able to put her
broken past behind her and create a beautiful future for
herself, her baby … and Erik.

***

Erik's mind whirled with possibilities as he stepped
onto the porch. Analise had skipped over to her
grandfather and given him a big hug. Erik's chest
swelled to see her so happy. *God, I love her*. She was

still all the things he'd admired ten years ago—intelligent, caring, compassionate, and fun. But now they were enhanced with experience. She challenged him, supported him, encouraged him, and made him a better person. Made him want to make the world a better place for her ... and their children.

They could build a beautiful, big house on the corner of his grandparents' property. It would have a large front porch with a covered veranda, a fabulous two-person shower in the master bedroom, based on their bathing experience of this morning, and lots of bedrooms for the inevitable results of their uncontrollable lust.

With the vision of a naked Analise still fixed firmly in his mind, he almost missed the note tucked into the front door of Gunnar's house. He carefully removed the paper and hesitated a moment before opening the letter. If it was for Gunnar, he could bring it down to the stables as soon as he put the bags inside.

His fingers froze as he recognized Brenda's handwriting and his name double underlined on the outside. The euphoria that had swept him through the last twenty-four hours fizzled and fell at his feet, replaced by the cool chill of impending doom. With the faintest hope that his ex-girlfriend had only written him a note to wish him well and to say she was going to live in Australia now, he opened the letter. She obviously hadn't returned to Toronto as he'd asked her.

His eyes scanned her message, and his heart started to fibrillate. She would be back after lunch—bringing Ian MacEwan. Analise's light footsteps on the porch alerted him to her arrival seconds before her arms wrapped around him from behind.

"Granddad's going to keep working on the barn. Want to fool around?" She slipped her hands into the front pockets of his jeans, which soon became too tight.

Shoving the note into the breast pocket of his shirt, he gently removed her hands before turning and wrapping his arms around her. "You have to ask? Don't you think you should rest, though? I don't want you to start feeling ill again."

"Hmmm, I'll rest later." She pulled his head down to hers, giving him a kiss that reached down into his heart.

He'd give anything to lose himself in her heat once again. To taste the intoxicating mix of love and lust that only she could engender. But Brenda was going to arrive any minute. And he was desperate to keep the two women apart.

"I can see I'm going to have to rethink my plan to work from home. We'll starve with the amount of billable hours I'll be able to get in."

"Maybe, but we wouldn't be cold," she countered.

He laughed, then removed her arms from around his neck. "I do have some work to do. A couple of phone calls to make."

"All right. I should sort out which photos I'm going to display at my exhibition." She caressed his cheek, then turned and walked into the house, but not without an exaggerated sway of her hips that tempted him to change his mind.

An hour later, Brenda still hadn't shown up. Erik

had tried to phone her in the hope that they could meet somewhere other than Gunnar's place. Unfortunately, her cell phone went straight to voicemail, and he'd been unable to locate Ian MacEwan. So, all he could do now was wait for the dastardly duo to show up and hope to diffuse the megastorm he could sense in the offing. The old cliché about a woman scorned flitted through his brain, and he clenched his teeth.

He took his laptop out to the porch. His last line of defense would be to suggest an alternative venue for their *discussion* before they even got out of the car.

"Do you want some lunch?" Analise lounged against the porch doorway. She'd changed out of her sundress and now wore a T-shirt and pair of shorts, showing off her shapely legs—legs that earlier that morning had been wrapped around his waist while warm water from the shower coursed over their joined bodies.

"No, thanks. I'm still full from that huge breakfast. Do you mind if I eat later?"

Once he sent Brenda on her way, he could satisfy all his appetites.

"I'm not hungry either. Just seemed the thing to do. I'll go take a couple of sandwiches out to Granddad. At least he seems to have regained his *joie de vivre*. Have you seen the stables? They're immaculate. When I left him to come back to the house he was nailing some loose boards back in place."

Erik followed her into the kitchen.

"I'll take the sandwiches to your grandfather and see his handiwork now. Why don't you have a rest and then we can take Gunnar out for an early dinner in Gimli? I hear there's a new fish restaurant in town. With the Icelandic festival over, it should be quiet enough that we can get a table without a reservation."

"Sounds great." She slapped together a couple of sandwiches and, after pouring some lemonade into a Thermos, handed the lunch bundle to Erik.

He gave her a kiss on the cheek before going in search of her grandfather. Following Gunnar around as the older man munched on the lunch Analise had prepared, Erik was surprised at the amount of work that had been accomplished in the couple of days since he'd last been at the stables. Ten stalls were ready for occupants, and the range of bridles and tack hanging on the wall were now cleaned and ready for use.

"Seems like you're ready to reopen," Erik commented as they sat on bales of straw at the entrance to the big barn, where he could still watch the driveway for any arrivals.

"Yes. Thought I'd start small, just boarding horses for now. I can add training and riding lessons later if there's a demand. Never thought I'd want to work again after I lost Lara. But with the next generation on the way, I thought I should leave behind something of worth."

"All my baby needs is your love, *Afi*." Analise's soft voice from behind him made Erik jump. "Although I'm pleased you found something to make you happy again."

"I thought you were going to rest." He put his arm around her waist as she stood next to him, her hand on his shoulder.

"I couldn't settle, too restless. Thought I'd wander out back and take some photos. Want to come for a walk?"

"You go ahead. I'll join you soon." He stood and kissed her on the cheek, then watched as she walked out the back door of the stables, her camera strap over her shoulder, a small satchel probably containing a few more lenses in the other hand.

He'd always considered photography to be an easy career, especially these days. Cameras were so sophisticated, you only pointed and clicked. But when he'd had a fleeting glance at the album Analise had presented to his grandparents at their anniversary party, he'd been amazed at the images she'd captured. She was a true artist and had managed to convey the very essence of love and hope onto the photographic paper.

The sound of tires crunching on gravel brought him back to the present with a start. If he wanted to ensure many more pleasant photo ops, he needed to get rid of Brenda and Ian as soon as possible. Gunnar turned around at noise of the arriving car.

"I think that might be for me," Erik said.

Gunnar looked pointedly at Erik's hands, which he was clenching and unclenching as though getting ready for a fight.

"Need some privacy, son?"

"Yeah, do you mind?"

"Not at all; use the house. I think I'll check the fencing on the paddocks, make sure none of the posts have rotted." As the older man wandered off, Erik spun on his heel and strode toward the car that was now stopped beside his own.

"What do you want, Brenda?" he demanded as soon as she stepped out of the car.

"Is that any way to greet the woman who, up until three weeks ago, you used to call sweetheart? The woman who washed your underwear and cooked your dinner? Oh, yeah, that's right. You replaced me. You found someone else, and you're already married. Tell me, Erik, does she know about your little pet project? Does she know that you still live so much in the past that you couldn't commit to a future with me?"

One wrong word, and this whole scene would detonate and take his happiness with it. He needed to reason with her. The logical lawyer he knew must be in there somewhere. "Brenda, you deserve a man who thinks you're his entire world. I'm not that man. We had nothing in common besides work. I could never have made you happy, not in the long run. You've got to see that."

"What I see is that your obsession with destroying this man here," she gestured at Ian on the other side of the car, "has led you to put aside your future, the wonderful future you could spend with me, and marry the woman *he* wanted all those years ago. You're so determined to destroy everything that he wanted or that he has, you've lost track of what you need. You need me, Erik. I'm the perfect wife for you. Instead, you married her, some little photographer who used to be the girl next door. Well, I'm here to tell you that without me, this," she swept her arm around the small farmyard, "this is all you'll ever have."

"Maybe it's all I actually need," Erik said, hoping to diffuse her tirade.

"See, you're still living in the past. When we first met, you said that ten years ago you couldn't wait to leave Manitoba and you never wanted to come back. Even last month, you said you were going to come here for three weeks, see your grandparents, then we were going to the Seychelles. That was your reward for putting up with three weeks in, and I quote, 'relative-filled Manitoba hell.' Are you telling me that in seventeen days you've changed your mind? That now you love it here and never want to leave? I don't believe you, Erik." She started to cry. The tears were silent at first but soon were accompanied by a high-pitched wailing. Erik didn't know whether he should try to comfort her or let her cry it out.

"Is that true, Erik? Is what she said true?" Analise's voice crackled with emotion.

He whirled to see her standing a few meters from him. She swayed once, twice, then fainted. Thankfully, his muscles reacted before his brain, and he caught her before she hit the ground.

Chapter Fifteen

A babble of voices sounded like they were underwater. Had she gone swimming? Analise wiggled, but something was holding her tight. Her eyes flew open, and she saw Erik's concerned face staring at her.

"Get a cool cloth," he demanded of someone as he lay her down on her grandfather's battered sofa.

A woman's legs appeared at her side. She followed the legs up to a Chanel suit, past a Hermes scarf, to the face of Erik's ex-girlfriend, Brenda. *Brenda, Erik, Ian.* Analise struggled to sit up, but Erik's strong hand pushed against her shoulder, holding her down.

"Easy, love. You fainted." He ran a wet towel over her brow, his hand shaking as he did so.

She pushed his hand away. "I'm fine. I just got too hot. I forgot my hat; that's why I came back to the house."

Ian MacEwan entered the room and put a glass of water on the coffee table, then stood back, looking as though he'd rather be anyplace else.

"Don't you think you should leave now?" Erik glowered at Brenda.

"I'm not going until I have some answers." Her tone was defiant with only a hint of defeat. The anger that had sustained her during her tirade against Erik seemed to have burnt itself out. Now, all that was left was pain and betrayal. Analise knew, because that's exactly how she felt.

Erik opened his mouth to comment, but Analise cut him off. "Yes, Erik. I think you owe us all an explanation. Please move; I want to sit up."

As Erik stood, she swung her legs down to the floor. The room spun for a moment, but by concentrating on the pinched face of the woman who sat opposite her, she managed to make it come back into focus.

Erik remained standing, his arms folded across his chest. Now it was his turn to look like he'd rather disappear.

Analise nodded at the other man in the room. "Hello, Ian," she managed after a sip of water. "And you must be Brenda."

Erik's ex was immaculately dressed and coiffed. Self-consciously, Analise ran a hand over her short hair, aware that it had been six weeks since its last cut, and it was now style-less. Brenda returned her scrutiny, and Analise could almost read her mind: "What does Erik see in her?"

No one seemed ready to make the first move. Brenda, having already said her piece, appeared to have nothing left to add. Ian stared at the floor as though to burn a hole through which he could disappear. Erik still stood defiantly at the end of the sofa, sharing his glare between Brenda and Ian.

"Ian, why don't you start? What's your argument with Erik?" Analise ignored her husband's huff and concentrated on the other man in the room.

"Got nothing to say, except, why me?"

Analise could feel Erik bristle from where she sat. His arms unfolded, and his hands clenched in fists at his side. If she didn't want her grandfather's sitting room busted up in a brawl, she'd have to diffuse the tension somehow.

"Why don't you start with what has happened since ... since school, and what you think Erik is responsible for," Analise prompted.

"With all the gossip about Karen's death, I couldn't get a decent job after school finished. Everyone blamed me. So I decided to start my own business. But he," Ian pointed at Erik, "made sure they all failed. I had to take a job as a garbage man in Gimli to support my family. Then, a couple years ago, things started to turn around. I noticed your grandfather was getting rid of his horses and cutting back. I've always been a good rider, so I thought I'd take over his business. Suddenly, the bank started lending me money, said a private investor was interested in promoting growth in the region. I bought land, built stables and a house for my family, got a load of horses, some from your granddad, others at auction. It was going good, when all of a sudden the investor pulled all his funds and demanded I pay back every penny within thirty days. It wasn't until Brenda here came to see me yesterday that I realized it was Erik's money. He ruined me on purpose. I have to declare bankruptcy. My wife is on the verge of leaving..." Ian put his head in his hands, his shoulders shaking in silent sobs.

Analise turned to stare at Erik. Guilt was written

all over his face, but still she asked the question. "Is this true?"

"Yes."

"And is what Brenda said true as well? Up until three weeks ago, you never wanted to return to Manitoba? Now, suddenly, everything is roses and you want to live here forever with me?"

"Yes. Am I allowed to make a statement in my defense?"

Analise sat back and crossed her arms over her chest to protect her aching heart. She'd let herself believe in the dream. That she could actually go back in time ten years and make a better life for herself and her child. Now she'd been deceived and lied to by another man.

He didn't wait for her answer. "Ian destroyed my sister. He selfishly took her innocence and threw it back in her face. He deserves everything he's gotten over the years. As for Brenda, yeah, I thought I loved her. I thought I wanted the big-city life. That a top-flight career in law could make up for a humdrum marriage. Then I came back here and met you again. Suddenly, everything I wanted became clear. I want to be known as a good husband and father. Good lawyers are a dime a dozen, but I truly believe I am the only man who can make you happy, Analise. Because I love you more than anything else in the world."

"How can I believe you, Erik? After all you've done the past few weeks is lie to everyone who loves you? Don't you think I've had enough deception in my life? Did you think you could hide all this from me?

You've sabotaged Ian's life and made me a pawn in your game of revenge. What did you think—that you could seduce me for old time's sake and rub his nose in it? Yee-haw, you got the girl he couldn't, congratulations. And for what? To avenge Karen's death? Let me save you three years and thousands of dollars. Here's what I learned in counselling: Karen had a disease, an illness. That's what killed her, mental illness. Not me. Not Ian. Yes, he did something stupid, but we were kids for God's sake. You can't hold us accountable. And anything you do now, or ever, isn't going to bring her back. It won't bring any of them back." Her voice broke, and a wave of nausea struck with such violence, there was no hope of quelling it.

Analise jumped to her feet and rushed to the toilet. When she emerged from the bathroom twenty minutes later, the room was empty except for her grandfather standing in the middle of the sitting room, looking like a Norse warrior. His cheeks were flushed, and fire shot out of his eyes. She hadn't seen him look so formidable since she'd first arrived and detailed her mother's treatment at the hands of her father.

"Where'd everyone go?"

"I kicked them out. This is my house. No one upsets my granddaughter in it."

"And Erik?"

"He's gone, too. If you want to see him that's your choice." He looked like he thought it would be a crazy choice, but he'd support her if that was what she wanted. Problem was, she didn't know what she wanted.

"You heard everything?"

"Yes. I saw you pass out and ran back here to check on you. Heard it all from the porch. When you went to be sick, I got old Bessy from the barn and reasoned with them to leave. Don't think your man would've gone if I hadn't threatened to put a hole the size of Lake Winnipeg in his chest."

Her eyes shot to the door where old Bessy, her grandfather's shotgun, sat ready to defend the house, and her, should it be needed.

"*Afi*, I need to go away for a few weeks— someplace where I can think in peace, with no emotional hangovers to haunt me. I've put some money in your bank account. Don't ask where it came from. I earned it. Trust me, I earned every penny. But I don't want it. Call Ian MacEwan—I think he might be interested in a partnership."

Her grandfather nodded, a hint of moisture in his blue eyes. "Will you be back?"

"Damn straight, I'll be back. This is my home, my baby's home. I'm not going to let some weasel lawyer and his fashionista girlfriend keep me away." Angrily, she wiped away her own tears.

"That's my girl." Her grandfather pulled her into his arms and hugged her until she stopped crying.

***

"Erik, there's someone here to see you." His mother's voice broke through the black haze that had gripped him since earlier in the day when Gunnar had pointed a shotgun at him and threatened to blow him away if he didn't leave.

He put down the pitchfork he'd been using to muck out the barn and rushed past his mother, not even asking who the visitor was. He'd left a dozen messages and texts on Analise's cell phone, hoping that as soon as she turned it back on she'd read them and agree to see him so he could explain.

Bursting through the back door, he let the screen door slam, willing to face the wrath of his grandmother in exchange for seeing his wife a second earlier. Instead of his grandmother's stern voice asking him where his manners were, he heard her offering a cup of tea to the person waiting in the front room. Erik paused when he realized the answering voice wasn't Analise's. But it wasn't Brenda's either.

Cautiously, because the afternoon hadn't gone well so far, he entered the front room. Having faced one shotgun today, he wasn't anxious for a repeat performance. His grandmother hovered near the sofa and excused herself as soon as she saw him.

Ian MacEwan's wife stood as he entered the room; he wracked his brain trying to remember her first name. Her brown hair was pulled back into a ponytail, and she wore a skirt and blouse that looked like it had been hiding in the back of her closet for quite a few years. She wiped her palms down her skirt before extending a hand to him.

"Good afternoon, Mr. Sigurdson. Remember me? I'm Melissa MacEwan, Ian's wife." Her voice wobbled, and her grasp was limp when he shook her hand.

Great, another woman come to tell me what she thinks of me. Perfect way to round off one of the worst days of my life.

"What can I do for you, Mrs. MacEwan?" Erik did his best to inject a note of helpful compliance in his voice.

She wrung her hands and stared at the floor. "I've come to beg you to reconsider foreclosing on my husband. Please, we have three small children. If we lose the house, we'll have to move back in with Ian's parents. I don't think I can take living with them again—all five of us in one small bedroom. If you give us a chance, we'll repay you as soon as we can." She sank to her knees on the carpet.

If there was any way for Erik to feel worse that day, he didn't know what it was.

"Please, get up." He put his hand out to help her to her feet. "Have a seat."

She did as he asked but still didn't look him in the eye. "Ian doesn't know I'm here."

"I won't tell him. Can I get you a cup of tea or coffee, Mrs. MacEwan?" He didn't know why he was prolonging this interview. Except he admired a woman who was prepared to fight for her family. Even if it meant humbling herself before a monster.

"Melissa, please call me Melissa. Yes, thank you, tea would be nice."

He went into the kitchen and boiled the kettle. Looking out the back window, he saw his mother and grandmother sitting in a set of wooden chairs, admiring the flower garden. He couldn't imagine either of them being proud of him right now. He wasn't proud of himself. Instead of the victorious feeling he'd expected, he felt shallow and petty. He'd ruined innocent lives in his quest for vengeance. And if he didn't set things right, he risked losing the woman he loved. His beautiful sister, Karen, wouldn't have wanted any of this.

He poured the boiling water into the pot his grandmother had left ready and carried the tray into the sitting room. Melissa MacEwan sat bolt upright in the chair, her eyes darting between him and the front door. He poured the tea and waited while she added a bit of milk to the cup. He should have offered her a Scotch. God knows he could've used one.

She took a fortifying sip of the hot brew before setting it down on the coffee table. Her hands shook less now, and finally she looked him in the eye. She had soft, brown eyes—Bambi eyes. Was it possible to feel worse?

"Ian has paid for what he did to your sister. When we were first married, he'd have nightmares about her. It made it hard for him to concentrate and get work. Finally, as time passed and more people forgot, it became a little easier. Still, he named our daughter Karen so he wouldn't ever forget. Said it was the stupidest thing he'd ever done and if someone treated his daughter like that he'd kill them. But, I hope you'll see, Mr. Sigurdson, by foreclosing now, it's not only Ian you'll hurt. I'm not asking for myself. I married him knowing what he'd done. I went to school in

Arborg, but he told me when we started dating, said I needed to know his bad as well as the good. It's the children, you see. We've already moved four times in the past six years. They love the new house, finally they have their own rooms—" Her voice broke, and she grabbed for her handbag on the floor, searching for a tissue.

Erik reached over, pulled the box of Kleenex from the side table, and put it in front of her. He might need one in a minute. He'd wasted so much time. For years, he'd only looked at the catalyst to his sister's suicide. He'd kept her memory alive for all the wrong reasons. Rather than remembering his sister for her beautiful personality, he'd focused on the horror of her death. It was as useless to blame the people involved as the rope she'd used to hang herself. He should have spent his energy assisting others—educating people and working to eradicate the stigma of mental illness so teens like his sister weren't afraid to ask for help. Instead, he'd made things worse, ruined other people's lives. Ruined his own life. But there was something he could still rectify.

"I'll tell the bank to hold off. We'll come to some sort of arrangement—maybe profit-sharing. That way, I won't burden the operating budget. Go home to your family, Melissa. I won't cause any more trouble."

"Really?" She raised her tear-stained face to his.

"Yes. I'll get the bank to call Ian in the next half hour." The relief on her face was worth the financial sacrifice. Chances were he'd never recover the money, but that didn't seem important now.

"You won't tell Ian I came to see you, will you? I mean, you can if you have to. It's just, he's feeling a bit emasculated lately…"

"I won't tell him, although I think he married an incredible woman. At least he made one right decision in his younger days."

"Thank you." As he stood, she flung herself into his arms, hugging him tightly.

"No need. I shouldn't have done what I did in the first place. I've made things worse and will probably pay for it for the rest of my life as well."

"I think your wife should be proud of you. It takes a big man to admit when he's wrong and try to fix it." Her hand flew to her mouth as though she realized that insulting him might not be the best thing to do in the circumstances.

He tried to smile to show he hadn't taken offense, but it was nearly impossible given the state of his marriage. Would Analise forgive him? Or had he inadvertently destroyed his own chance at happiness? "Good-bye, Melissa. I wish you all the best."

She climbed into a battered pickup truck and drove slowly down the driveway. As she turned onto the road he went into the kitchen and made a couple phone calls—the first to the bank, then to leave another message on Analise's phone. It had been only three hours and already he ached to see her. It was going to be a long evening.

Chapter Sixteen

Erik took the stairs two at a time. The old Paris apartment building had seen better days, although it was clean enough. Hell, he'd seen better days. It'd been six weeks since he'd held his wife, and he didn't know how much longer he could endure. Hope that she'd listen and take him back was the only thing that kept him going. And even that was fading now.

Stonewalled by Gunnar, Erik had had to track down Analise's father to find out her address. Monsieur Tagan had to call his lawyer to find out exactly where she lived. What father didn't even know his daughter's address? Then again, what husband lost his wife after only two days of marriage? The familiar ache in Erik's chest intensified.

He slowed as he approached Analise's floor. If only he'd gone straight back to Gunnar's farm after Melissa MacEwan had left. He should have braved the shotgun to explain to her. Instead, he thought he'd give her the night to calm down and had presented himself at dawn. He hadn't believed her grandfather's word that she'd already left. Only after searching the house and finding all her stuff gone had the reality of his situation hit him. Then panic had set in. As a world traveler, Analise could have gone anywhere. And Gunnar had been no help. He said his first allegiance was to his granddaughter, and until she gave him permission to divulge her whereabouts, he wasn't going to say a thing.

Yesterday, he'd seen an advertisement for her photographic exhibition at the Hôtel de Ville but she hadn't been there. What he had found, though, was some of the most moving photographs he'd ever seen. Analise had a gift for finding the humanity in even the most inhumane situations. He hoped she'd be able to find enough compassion in herself to listen to him. Because he couldn't go on for much longer without her.

His heart was racing by the time he got to the seventh floor. It wasn't from the exertion of flying up the stairs, however, but from the possibility of seeing his wife face to face. He banged on her door for several minutes to no avail. Unwilling to be defeated yet again, he sat on the floor, his back to the door, waiting for her return. He kept his eyes on the stairwell in case she saw him first. He wasn't going to risk her fleeing before they could talk.

Half an hour passed before he heard light, weary footsteps on the wooden staircase. He tensed and stood, rehearsing yet again what he wanted to say, although he was pretty sure that despite his preparation, all that was going to come out of his mouth at seeing her was a string of begging pleas.

A dark head appeared around the corner, and his heart leapt, only to fall flat on the floor as he realized it wasn't Analise. The woman was at first startled to see a man at the end of the corridor. She extricated her phone from her bag and pressed a couple of numbers before she advanced on him.

A torrent of French followed, and she gestured wildly. Unable to keep up with the rapid-fire tirade, he put his hands up in front of him in the international sign for surrender. Surprised, she stopped for a moment.

"*Parlez-vous anglais?*" He used one of the few phrases he remembered from school, asking if she spoke English.

"Yes, I speak English. Who are you? What do you want?" She had one hand on her hip and waved her phone at him with the other.

"Do you know Analise Thordarson?"

"I ask the questions, or I call the police and let them question you."

"My name is Erik Sigurdson. I'm Analise's husband—"

"She is not married."

"She is. We were married in Canada six weeks ago. I have our marriage certificate with me if you want to see it."

Wordlessly, the Frenchwoman held out her hand. Erik pulled the document out of his pocket and handed it over to her. She examined the paper carefully, then passed it back to him.

"Analise did not tell me she got married. Although, that would account for her sadness. I thought you were another one of those government men come to interrogate her."

"Government men have been interrogating her?" Erik's protective hackles rose. He should have been here to defend her. She'd asked for his help, and he hadn't even done that. So far, he was proving to be the worst husband. Ever.

"They stopped now. Probably something to do with that other man she used to see. I always told her he was too slippery. You must be the same or she would be with you." She shook her head as if to say that some women never learn.

"I'm not slippery. However, I am an idiot. I did something very stupid, and she ran away before I could explain and tell her that I fixed it. Please, do you know where she is? I need to see her." The desperation in his voice must have got through to the woman because her face softened.

"It is good for you that I am a romantic woman. I will call her and see if she is still in Paris. She sold her apartment and moved out yesterday. I offered for her to stay with me, but she said she had other friends," the woman explained as she dialed.

Erik couldn't follow the phone conversation that ensued in rapid French. That was going to be his first priority when he got back to Manitoba. Learn French so he could understand Analise when she was upset with him. The woman snapped her phone shut and raked him with her gaze.

"She says you are stupid yet not dangerous. She is at the Eiffel Tower, third level, saying good-bye to Paris. If you want to see her, you are to go there."

Saying good-bye to Paris? If she moved on, he'd have no way to find her. His heart raced. He had to get there before she left.

"Right. Thanks. I appreciate it." He sprinted for the

stairs; the woman's laughter followed him down the first two flights.

***

Analise hugged herself, although she wasn't cold. This was her favorite view of Paris. To see the grandeur of the city from a height where you felt you were part of it. She'd hoped that coming here would give her some peace. Of all the places she'd lived, Paris had been home the longest. Except the noise, the pollution, the social unrest, the threat of terrorist attacks disturbed her more than soothed. She longed to be back in Manitoba—where you could see for miles and not have another single person in your view if you chose.

A warm breeze blew her hair against her face and flattened her dress against her belly, which now had a tiny bump. She ran her hand over the evidence that her baby was growing. If it weren't for her pregnancy and knowing that she was solely responsible for the little life, she would have crawled into bed and stayed there for the next six months. Losing Jean-Claude had been bad. But the inevitability of what she'd long expected could happen had helped her deal with that blow. It was the sudden revelation of Erik's duplicity, especially so soon after she realized she loved him, that hurt the most.

And now he was coming to say good-bye. She shouldn't have run away, but she'd needed time to think about what she wanted, what she needed, before she saw him again. He was probably delivering divorce papers or wanting to discuss some sort of settlement. Well, he could go through her lawyer, keep it all professional. She could survive on her own. As if to reassure herself that all was going to be okay, she rubbed her baby bump again and stared out at the view of Paris in the evening.

The Tower wasn't too busy. As it was dinner time, most tourists were busy stuffing their faces with escargot or *coq-au-vin*, or trying to decide which was the best *prix fixé* meal deal. The distant sound of horns blaring from the streets below would always remind her of Paris. Not that she'd be gone forever. Her baby was French; she'd have to make sure they came to Paris often. And she was kind of looking forward to telling her father he was a granddad, especially as his new wife was only in her early 30s.

She saw Erik before he saw her, and her traitorous body wanted to run into his arms. She'd forgotten how tall and handsome he was. No, she'd not forgotten. She could still remember the security she'd felt when he took her in his arms. The way his heart beat under her cheek and his breath ruffled the top of her hair. He stepped off the elevator and stopped, hugging the steel frame.

Zut, she'd forgotten he was afraid of heights. Well, it sucked to be him, because if he wanted to talk to her, he'd have to come over to the edge—she wasn't going to make this easy for him. When his eyes met hers, she had to lace her fingers into the iron mesh railing. Every cell in her body was straining to throw herself at him. Her lips parted in anticipation of his kiss. Damn body, it was supposed to be on her side.

He took four hesitant steps toward her then stopped. She wasn't sure if it was his acrophobia or that he was unsure of her reaction. At least he wasn't holding out an envelope of papers for her to sign, ending their marriage.

"*Bon soir*, Erik. Welcome to Paris."

"Analise." Her name seemed wrung from him.

He took two steps closer, and she could see the pain in his expression. She should relent and move from the edge. Searching his face, however, she saw his focus wasn't on the view or the long way down, but on her. He seemed oblivious to his position so far above the ground.

"This is convenient," Analise said. "I can say good-bye to both Paris and you on the same evening. Twice the closure."

His eyes closed when she mentioned good-bye, opening only when she'd finished.

"I won't ever say good-bye, my love."

Confused, she took a step toward him so she could read his eyes. "Why are you here, then?"

"To beg you to give me another chance."

He sank to his knees. Several people stopped their sightseeing to watch the drama playing out before them.

"Erik, I—"

"Please, Analise. I was a complete ass. I was living in the past, thinking I could fix it. I thought if I avenged Karen's death, I would prove myself a worthy brother. The second I saw you again, all the feelings I had for you came flooding back. Only this time they weren't the emotions of a college boy, but the raging desires of a man. I tried to reason with myself that once I had you, it would be enough. When I found out you were pregnant the one thing I wanted was to protect you and care for you and the baby for the rest of your life. So I rushed you into marriage, hoping that in time you'd come to love me as I love you."

"Erik—" Her chest was so full she thought it might burst.

"Wait, before you say anything. Please, give us another chance. I still want to be a father to your child. I want to be your husband, to hold you every night and wake next to you every morning, to rejoice over the good and comfort you over life's disappointments. We are so good together, Analise. We could have so much happiness. Please…"

She reached out and touched his face before motioning for him to rise. His hands lifted from his side then fell back.

"What Brenda said—"

"Was mostly the ranting of a scorned woman… The reason I didn't like going back to Manitoba was because it reminded me of all I had lost—Karen and you. And despite what Brenda said and you may think, I never wanted you because Ian did. I've *always* wanted you, from the first time Karen introduced us. I will always want you. You're my woman, Analise. Time will never change that."

"And the past?"

"Losing you again, I realized it's the now and the

future that matters. I can't fix the past, but I can learn from it. And the biggest lesson I've learned is that I can't let you go again. I won't say good-bye, my love. I will follow you to the ends of the earth, live in a tent in the dessert or the top of a Nepalese mountain if that's where you are."

"That sounds a bit obsessive."

"I am obsessive. I can't live without you, Analise. The past six weeks have been my own personal hell, not knowing where you were, not knowing if you're safe. If you don't want me…" His voice trailed off as if finishing the sentence were impossible.

"I've been doing some thinking, as well, the past few weeks." She saw him take a deep breath in and then hold it as though bracing himself. "And I've discovered that I want to be where everything reminds me of you. If I can't have you, I was going to have the next best thing—memories of you. I'm done running. I'm booked on a flight back to Winnipeg in three days' time. I want my little Sigurdson," she rubbed her belly, "to know his or her family. I've had an exciting career and adventurous life; now I want stability and permanence. Do you think you can give me that?"

"Every single second of my life. But more importantly, I can give you so much love, you'll wonder how you lived without it."

Love radiated through her body. "Then let's go home, Prairie Boy."

Epilogue

Analise took three quick photos of the child atop the chestnut quarter horse. The rapture on the little girl's face as *Afi* led the animal around the corral was the focus of her lens. The child's mother was taking a video. But her camera was intent on catching all the action, and she missed the intense emotion of the moment. Analise pressed the shutter button until she became aware of a presence behind her. She turned her head to see her husband and baby standing a meter away. Lowering her camera, she beckoned them forward.

"Sorry, I didn't mean to interrupt," Erik apologized with a kiss to her upturned face.

"I got what I wanted. I think the mother will be very happy. And how's our little Lara doing?" Analise slung her camera on her back and lifted her six-month-old baby girl from the carrier strapped to Erik's chest. She gave one rosy cheek a loud kiss and was rewarded with a delighted squeal from her daughter.

"She's doing well. We tried a little rice cereal at lunch."

"So I see from your shirt. I hope you didn't have any client videoconference calls."

"No. And even if I did everyone knows being a good husband and father is my first priority. I did get something done though while Lara napped. I completed the registration of the Karen Sigurdson Memorial Foundation Promoting Mental Health."

"That's such a wonderful way to honor her memory."

"I only wish I'd done it years ago." Erik kissed his daughter and then nuzzled Analise's neck. "I thought Ian was working the stables today, not your grandfather."

"Ian is meeting with some marketing people to start an advertising campaign. *Afi* hates those business meetings. He just wants to be with the horses and the children, so he gladly switched places with Ian."

"As long as everyone's happy," Erik said.

Afi waved good-bye to the mother and child, who was animatedly telling her mother how tall the horse was and how far away the ground had been when she was on its back. Analise smiled. Her grandfather was as robust as he'd been in his prime, his thunderous laughter a common sound around the farm. When Lara saw him approach, she held out her little pudgy arms to her great-grandparent, who took her willingly.

"I swear she looks more and more like my Lara every day," *Afi* said. He held the baby up in the air above his head, much to her delight. "I'm going to tell you all about your great-*amma* when you're old enough to remember," he promised the little girl.

Analise laughed. *Afi* claimed the baby looked like her grandmother, but with her raven hair and green eyes she was almost the opposite of her blond, blue-eyed great-grandmother. Fortunately, she looked enough like Analise that no one had wondered why she wasn't fair like Erik. One day, she'd have to tell her baby who her real father had been. For now, Erik was filling in that role with so much love and enthusiasm, no one had even questioned whether he was the biological parent or not.

Afi carried Lara over to the horse, keeping her far enough away that she could see it without touching. He spoke to the little girl in Icelandic, and she babbled back, mimicking his tone.

"Thought you might be interested in this article in the paper." Erik pulled a folded page from his back pocket and handed it to her.

Anonymous Donor Gifts US$10 Million to Save the Children.

She glanced at Erik. They'd never discussed the Cayman Islands bank account Jean-Claude had left for her. She'd tried to talk to him about it, but he said he wanted none of it. He was happy providing for his family with what he earned as a lawyer. It was her money, she could do with it as she wanted. She'd never been comfortable with it, though, knowing that somewhere, someone had been hurt or killed in its acquisition. So she'd done the best thing she could—she'd given it away.

"You're okay with this, aren't you?"

"Absolutely. I've got everything I could ever want

or need right here." He pulled her back against him, wrapping his arms around her as they listened to the laughter of their child.

"So do I, Prairie Boy. So do I."

Thank you, reader

I hope you enjoyed reading Erik and Analise's story as much as I enjoyed writing it. If you did, please help other readers find it by leaving a review at your favorite retailer. Your review doesn't have to be long, but your opinion matters to me and other readers.

If you'd like to find out about upcoming releases, contests and events, please sign up for my monthly newsletter at https://alexia-adams.com. You can also interact with me on Facebook (https://www.facebook.com/AlexiaAdamsAuthor) and Twitter (@AlexiaAdamsAuth) or, of course, get in touch with me via my website (https://alexia-adams.com).

I love to hear from readers, so don't be shy.

About the Author

Alexia Adams was born in British Columbia, Canada, and traveled throughout North America as a child. After high school, she spent three months in Panama before moving to Dunedin, New Zealand, for a year, where she studied French and Russian at Otago University.

Back in Canada, she worked building fire engines until she'd saved enough for a round-the-world ticket. She traveled throughout Australasia before settling in London—the perfect place to indulge her love of history and travel. For four years, she lived and traveled throughout Europe before returning to her homeland. On the way back to Canada she stopped in Egypt, Jordan, Israel, India, Nepal, and of course, Australia and New Zealand. She lived again in Canada for one year before the lure of Europe and easy travel was too great, and she returned to the UK.

Marriage and the birth of two babies later, she moved back to Canada to raise her children with her British husband. Two more children were born in Canada, and her travel wings were well and truly clipped. Firmly rooted in the life of a stay-at-home mom, or trophy wife, as she prefers to be called, she turned to writing to exercise her mind, traveling vicariously through her romance novels.

Her stories reflect her love of travel and feature locations as diverse as the windswept prairies of Canada to hot and humid cities in Asia. To discover other books written by Alexia or read her blog on inspirational destinations, visit her at https://Alexia-Adams.com or follow her on Twitter @AlexiaAdamsAuth

Other Books by Alexia:

Love in Translation series:

Thailand with the Tycoon

Will being trapped in a failing resort change more than their itinerary?

When his older brother suffers a heart-attack, Caleb is sucked back into the family's virtually bankrupt hotel business. He reluctantly travels to Thailand to evaluate a last-chance resort with the help of a translator. Getting stranded with an enchanting local was not on the agenda. Neither was falling in love.

To read an excerpt visit my website:
www.alexia-adams.com

Bali with the Billionaire

He's all business. Until she makes him her business.

Ever since tragedy shattered Harrison Mackenzie's life, he's locked passion away to focus on work. Until a captivating woman without boundaries crashes through his meticulously constructed barriers to reach the billionaire's broken heart. Is he finally ready to risk loving again?

Vintage Love series:

The Vintner and The Vixen

After witnessing a murder, Maya Tessier needs to disappear. So she escapes to the cottage in France she inherited from her great-grandmother where she hopes to start a new life and concentrate on her art. Jacques de Launay doesn't like strangers on his estate, especially when they're a sexy redhead who reminds him of all he's lost. But if he lets her stay, more than his heart may be at risk.

The Playboy and The Single Mum

Single mother Lexy Camparelli must accompany super sexy Formula 1 driver Daniel Michaud for the rest of the race season as part of her job. Will she be able to keep her life on track and her heart from crashing or will the stress of living in the spotlight jeopardize custody of her son?

The Tycoon and The Teacher

Argentinian tycoon Santiago Alvarez will do whatever it takes to keep custody of his niece Miranda—even if it means marriage to the woman who jeopardizes his peace of mind. Genevieve Dubois is finding her way again after a traumatic experience left her unable to teach in a classroom. Helping an eight-year-old girl come to terms with the loss of her parents is challenge enough without the continual distracting presence of the sexy uncle who refuses to love. Then she discovers the real reason Santiago wants to retain guardianship of Miranda and it threatens all their futures.

To read an excerpt visit my website:
www.alexia-adams.com

The Developer and The Diva

Para siempre means forever. That's what they'd promised one another. Then she left. Now she's back, and para siempre is just two words written on the wall of the community center he's determined to tear down … and she wants to save. Will the pain of the past be too much to overcome, or will they gamble again on a love to last para siempre?

To read an excerpt visit my website:
www.alexia-adams.com

Guide to Love series:

Miss Guided

Mystery writer Marcus Sullivan is determined find someone for his younger brother Liam. Playing matchmaker on holiday in St. Lucia, Marcus tries to interest Liam in a beautiful local tour guide Crescentia

St. Ives. Then Marcus gets stranded with Crescentia and the plot to match her with his brother quickly incinerates in the flames of lust. No way can Liam have her when Marcus can't keep his hands off. Too bad he can't write a happier ending to their blossoming romance.

To read an excerpt visit my website:
www.alexia-adams.com

Played by the Billionaire

Internet security billionaire, Liam Manning, made a promise to his beloved brother, Marcus, to complete his mystery-romance manuscript. Problem is that Liam's experience with women is limited to the cold-hearted supermodels he usually dates. So falling back on his hacking skills, he infiltrates an online dating site to find a suitable woman to teach him about romance—regular guy style. What he didn't expect was for the feelings to be so...real. Can Liam finish the novel before Lorelei discovers his deceptions and, more critically, before she breaches the firewall around his heart?

To read an excerpt visit my website:
www.alexia-adams.com

His Billion-Dollar Dilemma

Simon Lamont is an ice-cold corporate pirate. But when he arrives in San Francisco to acquire a floundering company and is accosted by a cute engineer with fire in her eyes, it takes all Simon has to maintain his legendary cool. Helen will do whatever it takes to change his mind, and if that means becoming the sexy woman Simon didn't know he wanted, so be it. If only she wasn't about to walk into her own trap...

To read an excerpt visit my website:
www.alexia-adams.com

Masquerading with the Billionaire

World-renowned jewelry designer Remington Wolfe is competing for the commission of a lifetime and someone is trying to destroy his company from the inside. He's in for more than one surprise when his unexpected rescuer turns out to be a sexy computer specialist with a sharp tongue and even sharper mind.

To read an excerpt visit my website:
www.alexia-adams.com

Romance and Intrigue in the Greek Islands:

The Greek's Stowaway Bride

Hoping to make it to North Africa to free her uncle, Rania Ghalli stows away on the yacht of Greek millionaire Demetri Christodoulou. But when Egyptian agents board the boat, she can either jump overboard...or claim she's Demetri's new bride. Demetri needs a wife to complete a land purchase so he agrees to play along—if she'll agree to a real marriage. But keeping the vivacious woman out of his heart will be a lot harder than keeping her on his ship…

To read an excerpt visit my website:
www.alexia-adams.com

Daring to Love Again:

The Sicilian's Forgotten Wife

Bella Vanni has accepted that her presumed-dead husband is long gone, so it's a huge shock when he knocks on her door and announces his desire to resume their marriage. She can't trust his answers on where he's been or why he left, and she certainly isn't keen to walk away from the life she's constructed for herself in his absence. But when Matteo's freedom is threatened, Bella must decide which is most important to her: everything she's painstakingly built or a second chance at a love that never died.

To read an excerpt visit my website:
www.alexia-adams.com

An Inconvenient Series:

An Inconvenient Love

With the Italian economy in ruins, Luca Castellioni can't afford a distraction from running his successful property restoration company. However, he needs an English-speaking wife to cement a crucial deal. When his British bride-of-convenience undermines the foundations around his heart, he's forced to restructure his priorities. Is he too late for love?

To read an excerpt visit my website:
www.alexia-adams.com

An Inconvenient Desire

Investment banker Jonathan Davis retreats to his Italian villa to lick his wounds post divorce, so his flirtation with runway model Olivia Chapman is just that. But when his ex dumps their toddler daughter on his doorstep, Olivia's assistance is a godsend that shakes up his world in more ways than one.

To read an excerpt visit my website:
www.alexia-adams.com

Business Trip Romance

Singapore Fling

Lalita Evans's father hired Jeremy Lakewood in the family's international conglomerate, and now he's tagging along as she oversees their interests across eight countries in three weeks. Will Jeremy risk his livelihood and all the success he's achieved to win the woman who haunts his dreams?

To read an excerpt visit my website:
www.alexia-adams.com